# High Noon at Starbucks and Other Stories

"Tonally complex and acutely observed, Richard Freadman's powerful stories take us into the inner world of conflicted men as they confront personal crises, and into the experience of the people with whom they share romantic, familial or fleeting relationships. Freadman's exploration of the effect of patriarchy on both women and men extends the reach of Australian fiction. Running through the volume is a comic element, transgressive as well as funny. These engrossing stories make for marvellous reading."

– Hermina Burns, author of *Bite of the Bluebottle*,
*Edging Them Out*, and other volumes.

## Also by Richard Freadman

*Eliot, James and the Fictional Self: A Study in Character and Narration* (1986)

*On Literary Theory and Philosophy: A Cross-Disciplinary Encounter* (ed. with Lloyd Reinhardt) (1991)

*Re-thinking Theory: A Critique of Contemporary Literary Theory and an Alternative Account* (co-authored with Seumas Miller) (1992)

*Renegotiating Ethics in Literature, Theory, Philosophy* (ed. with Jane Adamson and David Parker) (1998)

*Threads of Life: Autobiography and the Will* (2001)

*Shadow of Doubt: My Father and Myself* (2003)

*This Crazy Thing a Life: Australian Jewish Autobiography* (2007)

*Jovial Harbinger of Doom: Short Stories of Laurie Clancy* (ed.) (2014)

*Stepladder to Hindsight* (2016)

# HIGH NOON AT STARBUCKS
## and Other Stories

### RICHARD FREADMAN

HYBRID
PUBLISHERS

Published by Hybrid Publishers
Melbourne Victoria Australia
© Richard Freadman 2023

www.hybridpublishers.com.au

First published 2023

ISBN: 9781922768155 (paperback)
9781922768162 (ebook)

 A catalogue record for this
book is available from the
National Library of Australia

Cover: Gittus Graphics – gggraphics.com.au

# Contents

*In memory of Roy Lionel Isles*

*1902–74*

# Starting Out

My mother, bless her umbilical soul, had a rule for everything.

"No moping in your room."

"Don't play at the Eltons'. A relative was in prison."

"If kids talk dirty, walk away."

So, when Raphael Grayson, a friend from school, invited me to join him and his father on a drive to visit his mother in Sydney, my mother was having none of it.

A thin woman with a pinched face, short wavy hair, and burning brown eyes, she shouted that at eleven I was *far* too young to travel with anyone but my parents. How *dare* the father leave it to the son to issue the invitation?! What *was* the father *thinking*?! What was Sydney to me, anyway? Why did my friend's parents live in different cities? Why didn't he live with his mother? Wasn't he older than me? What if my asthma flared up on the drive, or I missed my family, or …?

My usually compliant father clearly sensed that a lot was at stake. To my surprise he sided with me, looking straight at his astonished spouse as he spoke. The niceties of the invitation were irrelevant, he argued. Mr Grayson was a respected member of the

School Council and a reliable man. The mother was apparently in "hospitality", a solid profession. Their family arrangements were their own business. Yes, Raphael was older, but by less than a year. This was a perfect opportunity for me to "start out" on my own life-journey.

At seventy-three I look back on that moment with a certain astonished and ironic admiration.

What he didn't know was that Raphael had shown me certain photos he'd obtained from a shop in Sydney, and that I hadn't walked away. I was itching to visit the place myself.

*

They picked me up on a Friday morning. It was school holidays. We'd be back late Tuesday. My mother, fear now trumping the poor woman's fury, gave me a big hug, holding back tears. My father, also looking moved, shook my hand hard.

Mr Grayson was smartly dressed in a black leather jacket and grey slacks. He had a perfectly straight parting in his black Brylcreamed hair. He greeted me more warmly than did his son. Raphael sat impassive in the back of the red, black upholstered BMW, sequestered under his Beatles hairdo. But there was a welcoming Coke and bag of chips waiting for each of us. We munched and drank and looked at the grey wet Melbourne streets and houses, then foggy green paddocks with cattle feeding in the rain. Sometimes huge lorries passed us, swooshing muddy waves right up the side of the car, and making it shudder.

Mr Grayson tried to make conversation, but Raphael would just kill every attempt with a "who cares?", or a surly platitude like "do the crime, do the time".

After half an hour of his father clearly felt the need for some solace, so he put on a cassette by the singer, Leonard Cohen. The first song he played sounded so crushingly doleful that I couldn't understand why anyone would listen to it for pleasure. I have never heard it again and have never wanted to; so my memory of that moment is a bit hazy. But I remember a bird in the title, a tramp-like figure telling the 'singer' that he should just accept what life has given him, and an attractive woman at a doorway telling him not to hold back on the pursuit of his desires.

"That sounds like shit," said Raphael. "What's he on about?"

"He means that you've got to find your own path in life, regardless of temptations and people who want to stop you being who you are. He's on about freedom inside you. A space no-one should invade."

This rang a distant bell for me. Maybe "starting out" had something to do with that?

"*No kidding!*" Raphael replied sarcastically.

That killed the conversation stone dead again. I took out a book Mum had packed for me, *Play Football My Way* by Ron Barassi, and started to read. Raphael just stared out the window.

A couple of hours later we pulled into a muddy little town for lunch. How I detest those glum Victorian country towns! Weeds sprouted beside the footpaths;

paint peeled off Federation survivals; people trudged along the pavement like zombies. I was beginning to experience a nameless, sickly, sinking feeling. I have a name for it now alright – depression.

We proceeded to the adjoining restaurant for fish and chips, Coke, milkshakes, ice cream. We all picked up. Mr Grayson said to Raphael, "Good to see you looking like a happy camper, son."

The boy just scoffed. The father's face fell. I thought my friend was a bit ungrateful, given that his father seemed to be raising him on his own.

*

It was dusk when we pulled into a cream brick motel with an arch and a parking space in front of each unit.

To an eleven-year-old, the room looked sumptuous: cream brick walls, a white ceiling textured like sandpaper, a shiny dark-green sofa and armchair, and a huge print of Van Gogh's "Sunflowers" on the main wall. There was a double bed, a single bed, and a stretcher bed Mr Grayson had ordered. He explained it was for Raphael because I was the guest.

For that same reason, I was to have the first shower. The tiny bathroom was tiled in green and orange. I locked the door, started to undress, and was about to turn the tap on when I heard voices coming through the wall.

"You ungrateful little so-and-so! I agreed to bring Charlie to make it easier for you, and what do you do? As usual you're behaving like a brat. Stop being bloody

4

rude to me in front of him, *and act like his host!*"

"I *am!* I'm talking *lots* to him …"

I turned on the extractor fan with the water to muffle the rest and had the longest shower I thought I could without being rude. I started to wish I hadn't come. My mother drove me nuts, but at least I felt loved at home. When I re-emerged, Raphael was looking flushed and made an elaborate, obviously hollow effort to be friendly. The sickly glum feeling was getting worse.

We adjourned to a nearby Chinese restaurant for dinner. Mr Grayson looked thoroughly miserable. We boys loved the sweet and sour fried chicken balls, but he said the sauce tasted like "furniture polish". Yet even he – poor man! – cheered up over the desert bananas and ice cream.

On the way back to the motel I slyly asked Raphael when we'd get to the shop with the photos. He said he had it all planned.

Soon after we went to bed, Raphael was snoring softly. I pretended to be asleep. I lay there feeling wretched, trying to think about football, and those photos.

Presently I heard a click and dialling on the bedside phone between the father and me. He was talking in angry whispers. The woman on the other end was almost shouting.

"Why are you even taking that poor boy to see that woman?!"

"Because she's his mother and everyone needs to know who their mother is. That's why."

"He's already met her several times and knows who she is. The more he sees of her, the worse it will be for him."

"Listen! I'm his father …"

"Yes, well I'm his aunt and God knows the boy needs …"

The phone clicked. The last thing I remember is Mr Grayson smoking a cigarette. In the dark it made his lips and nose glow red.

Tearfully I resolved to ask him in the morning to ring my parents and suggest they collect me at the motel.

*

Next morning, a hearty breakfast and better humour all-round banished such thoughts. When Sydney's skyline finally materialized like inverted dominoes in the mist, Mr Grayson cried out, "Look at that, boys! One of the world's great cities!"

"Wow!" I said, starting to get excited. This is what I'd come for. Well, one of the things.

Raphael craned his neck to see and managed, "Cool!", but I noticed he was digging his nails into his palms, sending his fingers as white as piano keys.

We checked into a stylish hotel, all timber panelling and marble, unpacked, and then drove to the mother's "hotel".

Granted, distinctions between "motel", "hotel" and "pub" can be somewhat elastic. I was later to realize that another term possessed of a certain elasticity is "hospitality".

Anyway, this was no hotel. It was a pub. The oak counter was polished to a honeyed gleam. The panelled wooden walls displayed photos of bronzed glistening men on jetties holding huge fish aloft. A little black and white tiled path ran along the base of the bar under polished stools. The carpet, which occupied the rest of the room, featured grey flowers and red dots on a navy-blue background. Patrons going back and forth had worn a little track in it. At intervals, brown hessian striations peeped through the blue.

A few people were sitting at little circular tables or in high-backed wooden booths. Well back, a man and a woman were chatting over a beer. The woman kept looking sideways towards the front door. When she saw us, she nodded to the fellow, who hurried away. She started to walk towards us.

What happened next has remained etched in my mind, I don't entirely know why. It was as if the vision of this woman moving, slowly and unsmilingly, arms by her side, towards the son she rarely saw, sent me into a kind of shock.

She was shortish and thin with a big bust. Her claret-purple hair dye petered out among ascending white fibrous roots. Most of her hair hung down to her shoulders; the rest was wrapped around her head like a threadbare turban. She had long, garish red fingernails and wore a matching red shirt. Her black leather zip-up jacket gave over to a short floral dress. I remember thinking how odd it was that these estranged parents both wore black leather jackets, and that her extraordinarily lined face looked like clay cracking in the sun.

When she reached Raphael, she held out her arms mechanically like a sleepwalker. He bowed his head between them but stopped just before his Beatles fringe could brush her jacket.

In a sepulchral voice, she said, "Hello, Raphael," and in a still deader one, "Murray."

"Julia," he replied.

She led us over to the table she had been sitting at and pulled up two extra chairs. She resumed her beer, downing it with big sluicing gulps. Mr Grayson ordered a coffee. Raphael and I had milkshakes.

Julia noted how much taller Raphael had grown and then asked, "So, Raphael, how's school?"

"Okay," he said. "School's school."

"And do you and your friend Charlie here go to the same school?"

Suddenly feeling terribly sorry for him, I tried to help Raphael out. "Yes, and we like doing the same stuff."

"Well, that's good," she said, "that's what friends are for."

She was twisting a table napkin hard in her hands. I noticed a red ridge on the inside of each of her index fingers.

The plan was for her to take us to a games arcade and then to afternoon tea. Next day we'd go to the zoo with her. Then on Monday she'd take us to the pictures.

After a while she and Mr Grayson got up and disappeared into a passageway next to the bar. She took a bright red purse with her. We heard angry whispers and then the snap of what must have been the buckle on the purse. We pretended not to hear.

Partly – but only partly – to drown out the noise, I again asked Raphael when we would visit that shop.

"On Monday after the pictures," he said. "I've got it all planned."

We walked to the arcade. When we got there the mother gave us a handful of coins each and sat down on a plastic chair near the door. Raphael went straight to the shooting gallery and proceeded to take aim at a creature called the Red Devil. Two girls walked over to watch, but he ignored them. I was surprised by this because at school, unlike me, he was popular and confident with the girls. I played Speedway, which was just like driving a real car. Every now and then I'd look over at the mother. She never seemed to look at us, but often glanced at her watch. She was chain-smoking and gnawing at her index fingers. Hence the red ridges.

Afternoon tea was a touch shy of sumptuous, but not to us. We feasted on Chiko Rolls, chips, desserts and lollies in a nearby fish and chip shop.

The mother asked us which were our favourite games in the arcade and whether Murray had given us some spending money. Raphael replied that he had. I said that my parents had given me some for the trip.

Then Raphael asked, "Wouldn't you like to have a house of your own, Mum, instead of living in a hotel?"

She blushed and shifted in her white plastic chair. "No, Raphael, lots of people don't own their own houses.

I think there are better things to do with your money."

*

On Saturday morning the three of us got a taxi to Circular Quay. Raphael and I took up positions at the very front of the ferry. The sea spray and the gentle thud of the craft on the waves were exhilarating. After perhaps ten minutes we saw grey shadows flashing through the blue only yards from the boat. Then huge, curved, glistening silver shapes rose up out of the water, arched their backs and dived down again. Dolphins!

"Whoa!" Raphael screamed. His hair was flying backwards in the wind. He was jumping and laughing and screaming at the top of his lungs. I'd never seen him so happy. Shouting, "I'm going to tell Mum!", he ran downstairs to the lower deck where we had left her smoking and drinking a beer.

When he came back a few minutes later the smile had vanished.

"Is she coming up?" I asked.

"Na. She says there's tons of dolphins in the harbour and she's seen them before."

It was one of many moments on that accursed journey when I felt very sorry for my friend. But what was I to say? Boys seldom spoke about their feelings and there was no vocabulary for the emotions in my home. The best I could do was something inane like, "Jeez – I wouldn't mind living in Sydney!"

That scene has often wormed its wintry way into my waking consciousness in the ensuing years. As have two others from that day …

Perhaps a quarter of an hour after we'd started our circuit of the Zoo, we passed three men drinking beer at a makeshift bar under a tent. One, referring to us boys, called out, "Hey, Jules. Didn't know you were the domestic type."

Julia pointed to a high wire fence with a sign saying CROCODILE. Two icy eyes just above the water seemed to be perusing us when she said, quick as a flash, "There's more brains in that pond than youse losers could rub together."

They laughed uproariously and, just for a second, I saw a smile sneak across her face. It was the first time I'd seen her smile.

We thrilled to the animals, but Julia constantly complained that her feet were killing her. We didn't mind because each time she'd sit down for a rest, a beer and a smoke, we'd get an ice cream, chips, Mars Bars or Cherry Ripes. It did seem incomprehensible even to an eleven-year-old boy that someone would wear wretchedly uncomfortable, high-heeled shoes to the Zoo. In later years, however, I saw a certain logic in this choice, as in the short dress that was apt to lift in the cool breeze.

Chimps were swinging on ropes, eating, poking, grooming each other, playing chasey, or just sitting and gazing into space. Raphael's mother looked as bored as she had at all the other exhibits. Then a baby climbing on the wire fence came over and stared right into her eyes. "Shit!" she exclaimed, jumping back. But the chimp kept looking at her. She started to smile and took a couple of steps forward. Now they were only two feet apart. The animal kept looking at her. Then they started playing. She'd take a few steps to the left and he'd follow her. She'd take a few steps to the right, and he'd follow her.

She was giggling now. "Look at this, boys, I've got an admirer!"

"Cool!" we both said. At last she seemed happy to be there with us.

But on our way back to the ferry she was her old self. Complaining about her feet. "Dying'" for a cigarette and beer. It was cold by then and, sitting in the cabin downstairs, none of us spoke.

Mr Grayson picked us up at the pub. We told him we'd had a great day and he was clearly delighted.

*

Next morning, we toured the sights in his car. We saw the great bridge from a little lookout, and the Opera House, its giant frozen sails seeming to crest the breeze. After lunch he said he had to put petrol in the car and attend a work appointment. He'd also get us money for the pictures. He dropped us off at the pub, told us to find Raphael's mother and ask her to order Cokes for us. He'd be back in an hour.

"Okay," Raphael said to me. "We can tell Mum we're going to the arcade and go round to that shop instead."

"*Yes!*" I cried, raising a clenched fist.

Inside the pub there were people – mainly men –

laughing and clapping, making a huge racket. There was a woman leaning over a man in a booth with her arms around his neck, kissing the side of his face. Big lipstick blotches festooned his cheeks like warpaint. Another woman was sitting on the knee of a gent, sipping his beer. Startled, I realized it was Julia!

When she saw us, she got unsteadily off the fellow's knee and began swaying towards us, an idiotic, almost ghoulish smile contorting her flushed face. Strands of claret-purple hair hung down her face and wafted about her painted lips. The poor wretched woman sounded as though she had marbles in her mouth when, having clumsily straightened her dress, she asked, "What are nice young boys like you doing in a plaith like thith?"

I had fallen again into wordless shock.

Raphael started to reply, but she cut him off and slurrily inquired, "Raphael, have you got any of that shpending money that … that your f-father gave you left?"

Raphael said, "I guess," and pulled a ten dollar note from a little zip-up pocket in his pants.

Just as he was handing it to her, his father came in unexpectedly. He took one look and said, "What's going on here?"

"I'm just lending mum some money. She asked for it."

Mr Grayson looked her up and down and snarled, "Is that *right?!*"

"Mind your own bithness, hero boy!" she said, glaring at him with bloodshot eyes.

And then he exploded. "You drunken fucking *slut!* You couldn't even control yourself for three days! *Three days!* You're a *total disgrace!*

"Well, I wasn't too much of a drunken shlut … for you, was I, wonder boy?"

The other woman giggled but most of the people in the room had gone quiet. Some were looking away. The chap behind the bar was readying himself to act.

"Come on, boys, we're getting out of here," said Mr Grayson, putting one arm around Raphael's shoulders and the other around mine.

By the time we got to the car we were both crying. Mr Grayson said, "Raphael, you get in the front please. Charlie, sorry to leave you alone in the back but we'll talk soon."

He drove a couple of blocks, turned into a side-street, switched the engine off and just sat there for a minute, taking deep breaths. "I'm terribly sorry, son. Your mother does care about you, but she's got problems."

As he said this, he leaned over to put his arm around Raphael, but the gears and the console only let him reach half-way.

Raphael tried to stop crying but couldn't. He spluttered, "What *sort* of problems?"

"She's what's called an alcoholic. She can't stop drinking alcohol. She constantly gets drunk, and when she's drunk she acts crazy."

"If she's all the things you said she is in the hotel," replied the boy, "why were you ever with her?"

There was a very long pause. Mr Grayson had withdrawn his arm and was sitting up straight now. Presently he said, "Son, that's a hard question to answer. It's one of those things that we should talk about man-to-man when you're a bit older. Sorry, mate, but now's not the time."

"Yeah, yeah," said the son, looking despairingly out of the window.

Mr Grayson suggested that we head back towards Melbourne that night, stay in a motel, and get to my place around the middle of the next day.

Before I knew what I was saying I said, "If you don't mind, Mr Grayson, I'd rather go straight home."

That sickly feeling was so bad now I feared I might throw up over the black upholstery. Those photos were the last thing on my mind now.

"Me too," said Raphael.

His father acceded.

We checked out of the hotel. Mr Grayson phoned my parents to tell them we'd be home early on account of a work emergency. Then he phoned Raphael's aunt and asked her to let herself into the house so she would be there when they arrived.

"I'm really sorry that your first visit to Sydney wasn't everything you'd hoped, Charlie, but at least there were some good times, right? The three of us will go to a movie in Melbourne soon to make up for today."

That never happened. I never saw Raphael and his dad again. Mum said they moved to Queensland. I've occasionally wished I could raise a glass with the man he became, and chat about that indelible journey – the "Hero's Journey", perhaps?!

Anyway, Raphael, saying nothing, kept staring out the car window into the dark as lorries flashed by. I tried to read *Play Football My Way*, but I didn't feel like it. So I just sat there saying nothing too, and there was no music to break the silence.

*

The sun had just risen when we pulled up outside my house. My parents almost ran to meet us. Both looked worried. They said hello to Raphael who just nodded, and thanked Mr Grayson for taking me on my "first big adventure".

In the living room, my mother held out her arms and asked, "So, how *was* your first big adventure?"

I said, "Pretty good."

Then my lips started to twitch and my eyes began to sting and I buried my head in her chest and sobbed.

# The Check-up

Kelton strode briskly through the manicured gardens. Artificial streams burbled under miniature wooden bridges. Teak park benches nestled beneath shade trees. Hummingbirds tweeted in the orange poplars. As he passed through the grand plate glass and chrome entrance doors, he mused that he could hardly have been in a nicer hotel.

The main thoroughfare to the reception desk was oak-panelled and lined with original artworks. A large postmodern chandelier comprised of jagged multicoloured facets of stained glass hung above the point at which the long passageway opened out into the great dome of the foyer with its circular dark wood welcoming desk.

Walking up to one of the staff, he inquired, "Which way to 3A, please?"

"Take the escalator," said a kindly lady of mature years, pointing to the left. Go to the third floor, turn right and pass through the double doors. There'll be a desk right in front of you; report in there."

This wasn't a hotel, it was a hospital in affluent northern Florida, one that aspired to the condition of a hotel. "Client-friendly" American medicine at its sweetest, he thought. Elsewhere, of course, in parts hidden from view, people were dying, undergoing treatment in degrees of fear, dread, pain and misery, but long years in places of unimaginable horror had pretty much inured him to suffering.

Kelton, a foreign correspondent for CBS, was there for a routine heart test. The company required everyone over fifty – he was fifty-five – to have one each year. This fearless habitué of dangerous places had just returned from two months embedded with peacekeeping troops in Darfur. When he wasn't reporting from war zones in a helmet and bulletproof vest, he was at his gym in Jacksonville, curating a long-cherished sense of invincibility on stationary bikes, treadmills, and weightlifting apparatus.

The postings were often lonely and required long hours in cramped quarters – tanks, tents, makeshift barracks – during which he would indulge that fascination with other people's stories that had first drawn him to journalism. He'd sometimes make jottings for a novel he hoped to write. Adept at finely-coded communiqués from behind enemy lines and an astute observer of people and their foibles, he fancied himself a literary wordsmith-in-waiting.

His parents, whom he seldom saw, were ailing fast in the old family home in Connecticut. Perhaps this is why the novelist-in-waiting found himself noting with particular interest the many elderly couples who made their way along the carpeted corridors or sat side-by-side in armchairs in the foyer or on thoughtfully positioned sofas elsewhere in the vast tasteful expanse.

Generally, one member of a couple looked much more seriously ill than the other. Often one would be labouring, the other in anxious or solicitous or dutiful attendance. He might be shuffling, head down, his hands clutching the handles of a walking frame, his face mask-like: Parkinson's? Dementia? Like Kelton's father, he might be strikingly well-dressed for one so unwell: crisp shirt and tie, smart patterned sports coat, well-ironed slacks. But everything was too large now. He had shrunk and so the coat hung off him like a scarecrow's, the slacks dangling disconcertingly over the sides of track shoes that were fashion's one concession to comfort.

The elderly gentleman might have a newspaper stuffed into the little pouch that hung from the front bar of the walking frame, but the other things – the asthma spray, the small soft cushion to support his lower back, the long shoehorn, the many-compartmented pill container, the box of tissues – sprouted beyond the zip line of his wife's bag.

Or the woman might be in a wheelchair which her husband guided, a touch anxiously, around strolling patients, sober visitors and staff bustling in pale blue scrubs. She might be well dressed, or might have given up the effort: easier, Kelton surmised, particularly if others had to dress her, to slip into a track suit? More comfortable too? One thing she would not compromise on though was her hair. Just like his mother. Perhaps the hairdresser came to her now, or maybe her husband took her there in the car, one of their regular outings? Whatever it was, her white hair was expertly sculpted. Not a hair out of place, and though her hands were shaky now, her heavy makeup had been applied with precision, perhaps with the help of a daughter who popped in on her way to work to prepare her for the day.

Kelton surmised that her husband, whose ringed finger gripped the wheelchair handle with pressure enough to whiten his knuckles, had been a fine specimen in his youth (not that she hadn't been, but it was hard to tell now). Well over six feet, clean-shaven, his greased black hair immaculately parted, he still looked lean, vigorous, determined. Kelton imagined him a "man's man", summoned from active retirement by what he might have called "the situation of my darling's health".

*

The chairs in the spacious waiting room, with its scenic windows and pastel prints and décor, were arranged in curved rows like an amphitheatre facing the bustling reception desk. Above it a digital screen announced CARDIOLOGY UNIT. Kelton checked in for his heart test and sat down. He took out his iPhone but didn't feel like facing the vast impersonality of the web, nor the rawness of communication with friends or colleagues. He put the phone back in his pocket.

He started to scan those sitting around him. A couple was seated at the far end of the front row to his left. When he looked more closely he saw that the wife – both were wearing wedding rings – was occupying the last chair while her husband was in a wheelchair beside and turned towards her. Her left arm was extended towards him. They were just in touching distance, the tips of their pinkies loosely entwined. Kelton thought of Michelangelo's deity infusing Adam with life. How ironic, he thought, in this context!

She was perhaps in her sixties, well turned-out, her grey-streaked black hair swept back into a bun. She was rather overweight, perhaps, Kelton thought, resorting to food for comfort. Her husband looked gravely ill.

What, Kelton wondered, might the man have? Probably terminal heart disease, or maybe a heart wilting under the assault of chemotherapy for cancer? But then he had a full head of hair … Maybe it was a wig? A small bottle-green blanket was wrapped around his torso and encircled his neck. He looked terribly thin. They both seemed lost in thought, as if marooned in the bewildering moment.

What had they done with their lives? Kelton retrieved the iPhone from his pocket, accessed a file he'd called "Writer's Notebook", and started to free-wheel, his thumbs flying across the keys as he began to luxuriate in his writing zone.

So … the guy in the wheelchair has been a diplomat, like the British Foreign Secretary I interviewed … Picture him decades younger. Thrusting. Radiant alpha health. A man of distinction? …

She looks smart. Composed amidst this desolation … Has been something too. Businesswoman?

Curve back to their early days? ... Met young, married early on the back of adolescent passion. Family life – travelling the world for his job. She the dutiful partner: managing the movings of house, the kids' often troubled adjustments to new schools and other children.

Or ... maybe she started her business when at last they settled and the kids were in their teens, perhaps in DC.

The history of their decades-old marriage? ... They bobbed along like a couple of that time. Career-driven guy. Roles held – until the kids left home? ... Or maybe the cracks appeared earlier. She got sick of the life of devotion. Demanded a life of her own in a place that was really home, near her friends and family, where she felt like *someone*, not just an accessory.

***AUTHENTICITY

He's furious as he writes. Model this on my breakup with Meg? Meg's parting tirade: "It's always other people's stories, isn't it?! What about *my* fucking story, *our* story, *jerk*?!"

OR: make it more about family._Parents agree the toll on the kids too great. They need security. Friends. Family puts down roots in DC. She can start her own career there. He can pursue his with less cost to family ... or so he tells himself.

But the marriage, now already battered, bleeding, held together with scar tissue [yes, go with that!] Huge resentment going both ways.

Note: I can do the career-obsession. No problems!

But kids? Refer nieces and nephews ...

Could go still further re female agency focus: she takes the kids unilaterally to DC. Puts down roots. He can join them or not as he pleases. The kids can visit him. Marital cold war now. Then rage, rage, rage!

Really bad stuff starts happening – climax or turning point in the story? Depends on narrative decisions I make re the above ...

He's never available in (Paris?) when she tries to call him. "Are you *fucking* someone?!" she screams down the phone, thinking (erroneously) that the kids would not hear. He denies it, point blank. But can she believe him? She rings at odd hours, trying to catch him out. But nothing. He agrees to keep his phone on at all times – except in meetings.

Or maybe he's the jealous one? Why, he wonders, had she been so incredibly anxious to get home? Sets traps to check her out like I did when Meg was pouring her heart out to that guy in Seattle. Finds nothing. But suspicion festers.

OR – you could tone the whole thing down. How un-American! Who the hell'd be interested? ... Maybe nothing other than the usual moods and tides of cohabitation down the decades. Basically a pretty solid bond? Have to be very granular to get that without schmaltz!!

So what's brought them here to Mayo Clinic in Jacksonville, Florida? Had they moved down here anyway, to semi-retire away from the icy winters up north? Or had something come up – a symptom, an aberrant test result – while they were contentedly settled in DC, the kids at college, or embarked on families and careers of their own … A medical catastrophe shatters whatever they had, whether by monitored degrees or in a blinding shock of diagnostic revelation. Perhaps they'd moved to be near Mayo, to be close to a specialist who was a world leader in what the man had.

So where now? His heart at the last frontier? Medical science buys him some extra time? NOW – does he cherish every moment? Upturn old toxic priorities? Or does all the old drive and restlessness flood back with returning health. Now she's grieving for a certain calm, attentiveness, connection that she'd guardedly allowed herself to hope for during the intimacy of his incapacitation [yes, use this!] … Always a forlorn hope, she knows.

But the main take is surely that he really is terminally ill. So then, cardiologist receives the report on today's test and says to them, sensitively enough, but as he's done to many others: "I'm afraid we've done all we can do. We've exhausted all avenues. Even if we tried to buy you a few more months with more chemotherapy, your heart would not stand it. It's my very unhappy task to tell you both now that from this point on we will have to regard your condition as palliative. We can give you the best quality of life in what remains, but we cannot, I am sorry to say, make that life last longer than your disease allows."

Now the next family gathering might be his funeral. How would she feel on that day? A great swirling mixture? Numb, distraught, wildly conflicted?

Depends on the above!!

Maybe …

\*

A nurse now appeared clipboard in hand, called Kelton's name and with a pleasant smile led him to a small, windowless white room with a speckled white linoleum floor, a narrow grey-blanketed bed and various pieces of apparatus along the walls. A treadmill with handlebars loomed over the rest of the equipment. She introduced him to Sandra, an unsmiling short, middle-aged woman with wavy cropped ginger hair who was to conduct the tests, then left the room.

He had gone on a long jog before the appointment to banish a twinge of anxiety that had made its unexpected way into consciousness, and to ensure his blood pressure would be spot-on for the examination.

Sandra wrapped the grey monitor cuff around his upper left arm and focused hard on a little dial as she inflated the cuff, then let the air hiss away. "Do you have high blood pressure?" she inquired.

"No, I've *never* had high blood pressure. Why do you ask?"

"Well, it's up a bit now. Might just be cuff pressure. Some people get it because they're nervous about a test."

"But I'm *not* nervous."

"Well, the supervising cardiologist will take all of that into consideration."

"So you're a nurse, I suppose?" he inquired.

"Used to be a cardiology nurse. Now I'm just a

technician," she replied in a tone so flat that he felt his blood pressure rise a notch.

She instructed him to sit on the bed and remove his shirt, then began shaving little clearings in his luxuriant black chest hair, lower torso and legs. Having attached adhesive patches and cables, she instructed him to lie down and breathe normally. She watched a little needle dance out wavy lines on a screen, printed out a graph and told him he could sit up.

"So how was that?" he asked, assuming that a cardiac nurse could read such a printout but knowing that she probably wouldn't comment.

"I'm just a technician. We just have to wait on the consultant cardiologist's reading of the results."

Presently she instructed him to mount the treadmill. As it gradually accelerated, he was to let her know if it was becoming uncomfortable. Now he was off and running, faster and faster, the vitality of a man of action flooding back into his body. He'd been on a hundred treadmills in gyms and hotels all over the world and there'd never been a problem.

"How are you feeling?"

"Good," he puffed.

"Okay," she replied firmly, "we can stop there."

He was surprised, but she was already decelerating the machine.

"So how was that?" he asked, knowing full well she wouldn't say.

"As I said, I'm just a technician. You'll have to be patient until the supervising cardiologist gives you his assessment. What I can say is that there is nothing in what I have said that should alarm you. We'll need you to take a seat again in the waiting room. It could be a little while, depending on how busy the cardiologist is."

She opened the door, her face a maddening imperturbable mask. He resumed his seat in the amphitheatre.

*

The couple whose backstories he'd sketched earlier were gone, perhaps still in a consultation or making their heartbroken way to the car park. He started to imagine how it would be for them now and going forward in the wake of whatever they had just been told. But he couldn't keep his mind on them. An odd, queasy feeling in his arms and abdomen kept bringing his mind back to his own situation, a "now" that he was enmeshed in. Picturing Sandra's mask-like face and hearing again that flat lifeless voice, he had to fight back an impulse to catastrophize. What would she know, anyway? From nurse to technician – that sounded like a demotion …

Presently, another woman in a white coat called his name and ushered him into a small windowless white room with a grey desk and three pleasantly-patterned chairs.

"Good afternoon. My name is Jennifer Sturgeon. Do you prefer Jim, James or Mr Kelton?"

He said Jim was fine.

She explained that she was a cardiological resident.

He wasn't clear what that meant, but his stomach had started to churn unnervingly, and he didn't feel inclined to ask.

She had a kind, long face framed by dark shoulder-length hair. She was poised and slim and looked wholly dependable. Her light blue eyes made welcoming contact with his.

As his discomfort spiked, Kelton found himself gazing at the woman before him not as a doctor but as a woman, imagining what it would be like to surrender utterly to that soothing presence, wondering what she wore under that white coat … and under that? He scanned her hands for evidence of her biography. Alas, diamonds sparkled on the wedding ring finger.

"So Jim, the supervising cardiologist has asked me to have a word with you. I don't want to alarm you, and I want to stress that there may be no cause for alarm whatsoever, but your test result is not quite what we were expecting and we would recommend further investigation. Having said that, don't jump to the conclusion that the result is something we were very much hoping not to see, because the fact is, we're not entirely sure of what it is we're looking at. We're actually a bit puzzled."

Kelton inquired how this could be, how often modern cardiology found itself bereft of explanations, and then, much to his own surprise, as if ventriloquizing for another self, "Are we saying I might have a life-limiting condition?"

"So," she replied pausing for a while before continuing, "there could be two ways of taking that term – limiting as in limiting what a person will now be able to do in a life that is not expected to be shortened by an illness, or limiting in the sense of a shortened life. We may not be talking about either of these things in your case. Without further testing we just can't say. That's why we are recommending further investigation."

He scarcely registered these words because he was now gripped by a fluttery tumult, with wild rushing sensations in his ears and a strange falling feeling, as if he were plummeting through space. Hot perspiration pricked his forehead. His hands trembled. His mind started to rewind earlier chapters of his life, as if in slow motion, though he knew that all of this – the tumult, the panic, the plummeting, the rewind – was happening in a split second.

What might his life have been like if he hadn't lived it on the wing? If indeed he'd paid more attention to Meg's story – to *their* story, come to think of it, to *his* story? His real, deep-down story. In a strange way danger had been his refuge. He'd wimped on the really hard stuff, the personal stuff, had taken flight, over and over, *literally*. Now there was no place to hide. Maybe he and Meg could have built something, a family, the miracle of being the most important thing in another person's life over decades? Shared stories, not the wintry, solitary, fabricating self …

He now realized that Dr Sturgeon was standing by the open door offering him her hand with a warm smile, having advised him to hold off from any demanding exercise for the moment and to ring the number on a card if he started to experience symptoms.

Shakey with anxiety and fatigue, he made his way through the amphitheatre, past blurred faces in the long corridor to where the chandelier swayed luridly overhead, and out into the gardens.

There in the shade of an elm tree was the couple from the waiting room, she sitting at one end of a wooden bench; he, the wheels of his chair resting in the grass, turned towards her. She was leaning over him, her chin resting on his bowed head, her right arm wrapped around his back, sobbing. He too was sobbing, leaning into her embrace, burying his head into her neck.

An enormous tide of compassion swept over Kelton. His own worries were for a moment no more consequential than a misplaced car key.

He stopped and asked, "Can I assist in any way?"

"Thank you," the wife said, lifting her head. "That is very kind. But it is not as it seems. The doctor just told us that there is a new procedure that will return my husband to normal health within a year!"

The man lifted his tear-streaked face and nodded in confirmation.

"That is wonderful news," stammered Kelton.

His Writer's Notebook came to mind, but as he fumbled for his phone he felt something giving way inside him and, having nodded farewell to the couple, wandered off to find his car.

# Solly, My Sister

It's late Friday afternoon and the temperature is rising. My father, Nathan, has just lit the first fuse. A small businessman, he's declared *yet again* that the Liberals will always have his vote because only they understand small business. My wife Sarah and I cringe.

"So," snarls my sister Solly in her deep, hoarse smoker's voice, "I s'pose you think the whole country's in small business *for christsakes!*"

Nathan's about to bite back when our mother, Esther, activates another fuse. "Come, dear, be a wise Solly and let's not have an argument before we light the candles."

"*Jesus!*" yells Solly, "Be wise, Solly. Be gentle, Solly. What sort of a *goddamn* name is Solly anyway?! What the *hell* were you people *thinking*?!"

Solly's existence has required of Esther a twenty-year apprenticeship in the arts of appeasement. She replies as usual, "Dear, as I've told you, when we were choosing a name for you, feminists were saying parents of girls should consider boys' names to avoid gender stereotyping. Not *really* boyish names, of course – not like Tom, Dick or Harry – but names that could work for both sexes. We liked Solly because Solomon was wise; and in Hebrew "solly" means man of peace. And Rabbi Gruner, a woman herself, thought it was an excellent idea."

"Well, good on you and the rabbi!" seethes Solly, storming out. We hear her beat-up old Mazda screeching down the driveway.

"Bloody fool," mumbles Nathan.

"You know she can't help it, dear," says Esther.

This scene has repeated itself over and over since Solly was a teenager. She's obsessed about her name. I don't get it. I mean, when all's said and done, what's in a name, anyway?

Yet no one will be more upset when Esther and Nathan go than Solly. She'll be absolutely devastated. She's incredibly connected to the family. She's like an alley cat that comes in for food, snoozes on the sofa, then disappears into its backstreet world.

The family's contoured to contain Sol's eruptions, her moody comings-and-goings. She knows she's safe with us, and, yes, loved, come hell or high water. And this elastic and nurturing little world allows her the illusion of living wild, counter-culturally, grittily, riskily urban.

The family gets plenty in return when Sol's "up". Then she's a huge hugger, warm, totally in your corner. When she's down, a shadow seems to pass over her face, and a second self – suspicious, hostile, delusional – takes over. Solly One and Solly Two don't seem to communicate. She's truly a divided self. From one hour to the next I never know which sister I'm going to get.

Solly's always, *always* late. One Sunday brunch we'd started without her. She appeared at the dining room door in a matzos-patterned dress from some gimmick shop in Glen Huntly Road. Essaying a Cossack dance and chanting, "Tradition!" she flew around the table throwing her arms about each person's neck and planting sloppy lipsticky kisses. "Booda booda boodiful!" she'd exclaim as each kiss made landfall, while the recipients, some reaching for napkins or handkerchiefs, grimaced in feigned amusement.

Absurdly sensitive to criticism – real or perceived – she can send herself up mercilessly. Her long, narrow white face is crowned by dark-brown crinkly shoulder-length hair, and her darting pale-blue eyes by thick blackish eyebrows which are apt to repeat themselves, much to her annoyance, in a feathery moustache above her thin wide lips. So hirsute are her limbs that she says she'll open a pub called The Gorilla Arms. Her heroine is Joan Rivers.

Solly and peace? Solly and wisdom? *Please!* Her signature tempo is hurtling. Sometimes when I'm in our parents' basement I'll hear her "walking" overhead, the floorboards thumping as fast as most people sprint. But the sprint's just the lap of an oval. She winds up where she started. Her life-trajectory is basically circular. Same mood swings and relationship problems; same inability to hold down a job, to persist with therapy. She's twenty-five now. Is there a cut-off age for making major changes?

A few years ago I had a dream about her. The family

is at Kunyung Beach on one of its Mt Eliza holidays. Solly's maybe nine. The tide is receding, leaving wet sand that she's using to build some sort of figure. A fierce dry wind is driving clouds of sand along the foreshore, getting in everyone's eyes, stinging shins, coating everything in its path. I shout that we should all go home and everyone agrees. Everyone except Solly. She's screaming and crying that she has to finish her figure. She's stamping her feet, flailing her arms. When Esther and Nathan make to leave she starts pulling ringlets from her head and casting them to the wind which sweeps them down the beach. The parents agree to stay. They set their umbrella against the wind. Solly goes back to work. As I look at it, the figure keeps morphing: now a snowman, a dybbuk, a scarecrow, a tramp … Solly is labouring desperately but the hot wind is drying the sand faster than she can build with it. Finally she gives up, rushes into Esther's embrace crying hysterically, beating her fists against Esther's arms. I am overcome by a horrible sinking feeling. I turn to leave. I take one last look at the doomed figure. Its disintegrating face is Solly's.

We're very different. I'm a straight-liner; a denizen of the destination. I'm the doctor Jewish parents dream of. Solly says that I'm middle-class suburbia "to the coils of your DNA", "someone else's idea of a person". She crows that Sarah is "buttoned-up like a bloody nun" and hasn't got the "spunk" to make an interesting life with me. We have screaming rows about her attitude to Sarah. She doesn't back off, but when she's with

Sarah she's all sweetness and light. I don't get it. Sarah says it's jealousy, but that seems a bit of a stretch.

Sarah actually makes huge allowances for Solly, but Solly only sees her in terms of herself. Pursing her lips and raising a hand with thumb and forefinger just touching, she flounces, "Sarah's so *demuuuure*. But if a woman like me who doesn't mind getting up people's noses says it like it is, people say, "Put the silly bitch on medication!"

There's something different about Solly's psychology, if that's what you call it. I feel like I've "got" a self, but Solly seems to have to build one, over and over again. And how does she go about it? The whole plan seems to be about not being like other people: not submissive liker Esther, not right-wing like Nathan, not "middle-class" like me, not "buttoned-up" like Sarah. But where's Solly in all this?

If I try to make even the most respectful suggestion to Solly – say, about completing her endlessly-deferred interior design course, getting back into therapy, or taking things slowly with her latest boyfriend – she'll seethe, "What would you *fucking know*, Michael?! My big brother the pathologist-Rebbe!" And she'll sweep her hands down from her cheek bones contouring a Hasidic beard.

It's even occurred to me that I married Sa, as I call her, partly because she's so unlike Solly; but could siblings be that important?

Solly's a powerhouse around the family, but that's her comfort zone. Once I organized a job interview for her at the pharmacy beside my rooms. I stopped at the window to give her a thumbs-up just before the interview, but she was lost in a world of worry: flushed, chewing her nails, checking her hair in her makeup mirror. She'd dressed smartly for the occasion in a white shirt, black skirt and shiny black shoes. When the pharmacist arrived Solly patted her hair, tugged at her skirt and looked overcome as she got to her feet. I've never felt so sorry for her.

She got the job but stayed only two months. She claimed that the female clientele were "total phonies" who treated her with contempt. "Those dumbassed fake blondes would marry anything with a Porsche, a pulse and a penis."

I reckon I'm a good listener, but fifteen minutes with Solly and my head hurts.

I once drove with her to a family wedding in Bendigo. The Mazda was an absolute tip. The back seat was a metre deep in old clothes, dead Coke cans, empty stubbies, shoes, crumpled notes and writing pads, airport novels, yellowing newspapers and traffic infringement notices. Before I could get into the passenger seat she had to scoop up two armfuls of junk and throw it into the back. Detritus came cascading down behind the front seats. An ugg boot came floppily to rest at the base of the back windscreen.

There must have been a hole in the exhaust pipe because the engine was guttural like a motorbike's and acrid fumes filled the cabin. There was a layer of sandy refuse at my feet – an old comb, a tampon, an empty water bottle, a crumpled Lotto ticket, a ten-cent coin, and a plastic brontosaurus which had liberated itself from her key ring. When the car hit a bump this noxious sediment would levitate, rearrange itself in mid-air, and settle again before the next jolt.

Her friend Miriam's husband, Morri, had returned home from an Asian golfing holiday with something that required three courses of antibiotics. "I told her not to marry that jerk. I mean, he was trying to hit on me before he hit on her at that party and he'd do it to the barber shop floor if it wasn't swept. But *oh no*, that was just Solly being cynical again and who was I to bloody talk with my kamikaze history with men? He made her feel *special*. He made her laugh and he was an old-fashioned romantic under that hard-nosed exterior, always coming up with just the right gift for special occasions – like the part-share in that ski lodge. But who was the fucking *skier*? Not her. *Him!* And boy, did he know his way around in the cot! I said as tactfully as I could, hello!, you don't learn those tricks on your Pat Malone. You learn them with other women. And anyway, it's not all about technique. You've gotta wake up with someone too. Not just fuck yourselves to sleep. I told her they needed relationship counselling. It's about a person you can bloody *admire!* Who will cherish you. That's when the chickens come home to roost – in the cold light of morning. Do they even play golf in Thailand? So now she's had – you know what, you know where and …"

"*Alright!*" I shouted. "I get the picture! Didn't it

occur to her that he was going on holidays without her for a reason and that maybe she should try to talk to him about the marriage?"

"*Look!* I told you I'd recommended counselling. What rock have you been living under for the last hour?! *Jesus!* I think you're listening so I keep explaining things, but you're off with the fairies! I don't know why I *bother!*"

Guilty as charged. As my head started to throb I had indeed tuned out; or perhaps branched out. I was picturing the nice wide hotel bed that would await Sa and me after the boozy reception.

I'm always worried about tuning-out when I meet Sol for lunch at the deli across the road from my rooms. Named – much to the displeasure of the local Hasidic community – "Bagels and Side-Lox" – it's nicely appointed and spacious enough for Sol to hold forth without my headache spreading to other patrons.

Today she was "up" – right up. Her welcoming hug just about cracked a rib and she was "dying" to hear the latest of Sa, the kids, my practice. She'd met a guy: Simon. He was "super-interesting and super-successful". He apparently lived in a palatial high-walled new residential complex just off High Street in Armadale. He ran a company managing elite athletes. He mentioned some footballer … Capper. Simon "looked a bit rough but had oodles of charm and a sensitive side … No doubt about it – there was a caring human being in there."

Just as I was tuning out she said something that

pricked up my ears. "He's got a wicked twinkle in those eyes and although he wants quality companionship he doesn't pretend that he doesn't want other things as well. When he took me to dinner the other night at Columbo's he told me a couple of gags that were even a bit fruity for *me!*"

So. What do I do? If I say nothing, she'll get kicked in the teeth again. If I say something, I'll get kicked in the teeth – and she might take up with this guy just to prove me wrong.

I said, "Look, sis, I know you think I'm a pompous twerp. An Old Testament Patriarch. But sometimes I say things because I don't want my lovely, warm, caring, smart sister to get hurt. This Simon might be the greatest guy who ever drew breath. I'm not saying he isn't. But if his idea of wooing a woman is to make kinky references to sex over dinner on one of their first dates, a red flag goes up for me. I ask myself, what sort of man would do that? Plus, what's this corporate high-flyer doing taking you to a down-market family pizza restaurant?"

"Well that's just fucking *typical, isn't it!?* Old Testament Patriarch. You got it in one! Columbo's make some of the best pizza in Melbourne, and if you came down from the clouds and looked at a few sex surveys you'd know that Simon is *by no means* Robinson Crusoe when it comes to those things!"

"Sis"...

"Don't 'Sis' me!"

"Okay, Sol. Look, I'm a pathologist. I spend half my

time looking through microscopes at bugs in people's body fluids. I've got a pretty good idea of what people get up to and I can tell you, in all honesty, that what they do between the sheets is of no interest to me so long as they treat one another okay. I'm just saying that a guy who runs that line over dinner early in a relationship – if that's what it is – is a good guy to take things slowly with. Check him out. If he proves to be a paragon, I'll pay for the wedding. I'm just worried that you might be falling into a bad pattern again."

"What fucking pattern?!"

"Taking up with lousy people who leave you for dead. Frankie. Dave. Gerry. Tony. Need I go on?"

"You sanctimonious son of a bitch! There is no fucking pattern!!"

"You're in denial."

"I'm not in fucking denial!!" She'd been glaring furiously at me.

Now, quite suddenly, she went quiet. It was as if a little film had come down over her eyes, leaving them glazed. I saw a tram plodding along Toorak Road glinting off her corneas. The silence went on for what seemed like an eternity.

Eventually signs of consciousness stirred behind her eyes. She glared at me in cold fury and snarled, "You and your fucking Jewish princess wife. I fucking *hate* you!"

She thrust back her chair, threw her napkin on the floor and ran to the door, grabbing the handle for an almighty operatic heave. But the door was one of those heavy plate glass Armadale affairs set in thick steel frames. The first heave almost dislocated her shoulder.

"*Fucking stupid door!*" she shouted. Patrons craned their necks towards the commotion while a mortified waiter helped her into the street.

I knew that my banishment would be of biblical duration.

I heard nothing from Solly for four months. Then, out of the blue, came a text message: "Long time no see my bro the MD. Fancy lunch at Bagels and Lox today 12:30?"

It was 12:20 now and I had nothing else planned, so I wrote, "Sure. CU shortly."

She was already there when I arrived. I could see she was "up" and, from the way her eyes followed me to the table, that she had something she was dying to tell me. "How's my *boodiful* big MD brother?! You look *great!*" Another rib-tickler hug.

"So, sis – how goes it?"

By the time I'd conveyed my linen napkin to my lap she was away. It was like nothing had happened the last time we met.

"You remember that guy Simon who manages elite athletes? Well, I finally got the big invite to his place in Armadale. We drove there in his black BMW. Black interior, black dashboard with more bells and whistles than the space shuttle. His apartment block is *ginormous*, like a castle with modern lines. It's got a security fence like Pentridge and everything's remote-controlled – the gate, the garage door. He didn't even need to pick up a remote control thingo – all the buttons were in the dashboard of the car! When we got in he put the door key behind a brass statue of a cherub in the hallway – marble floors, white walls, a *humungous* chandelier, not much furniture or decoration, though – and showed me the pool room and the state-of-the-art chrome and smoked glass kitchen. I'd baked some blueberry muffins for the occasion and after I'd put them down in their plastic shopping bag on the black glass table in the kitchen he took me up this spiral white-carpeted staircase to the bedroom. When he disappeared into the en suite and came out in a big white fluffy towelling dressing-gown and nothing else, holding two glasses of champagne, I said to myself, *Woah, this guy doesn't muck about!*

"I was feeling a bit nervy, a bit disoriented. So I tossed a couple more glasses down and then he told me to get my gear off and get into bed. *What the hell*, I thought. *I haven't been laid since the Ice Age*, and soon it was down to business. And I mean *business!* This guy's approach was feeling-free and fun-free! His technique must have been patented by Tokyo Robotics! Erogenous zones all accounted for? Check. It was like when I broke my ankle and the x-ray nurse drew a blue target X on one side of the foot, focused the beam on the X, then did the same on the other side of the foot, then rolled me over onto my tummy to focus on the X on my heel. Now there's precision for you!

"Well, by the time Robo-Lover trained the beam to the map of Tassie I was feeling about as erotic as a piano leg. *Dear God, let this be over!*, I kept saying to myself. So what if I'm an atheist? I feigned the best come I could and straight away his big hairy back sank down onto me and he started snoring like a Harley Davidson. I waited for him to tip a bit to one side then slid out and lay on my back thinking, thinking, thinking, and there was a feeling in my tummy like being told to dig your own grave. So I got up, put on his huge bloody dressing gown and had a look around.

"There were several other rooms off the passageway with its oldy-worldy white balustrade on the same level as the chandelier. First was a home entertainment room. Black walls. Black screens. Black leather chairs. Black stereo speakers. Black curtains. Next was the gym with exercise bike, weights, treadmill, and other gear I'd never seen before. The last was his study. Creeping in there I felt like Bluebeard's latest wife looking into the closet, but I wasn't about to stop now. I felt I was just getting the hang of this jerk. As I walked in there was a big framed photo of some meathead, sprinkled with confetti, holding a premiership cup in the middle of the MCG signed 'to Si-Guy – world's greatest manager'. The Robot must have been some sort of sportsman himself because there were more trophies than books on the shelves. But it looked like he did actually do some work at the desk because there was a big spreadsheet thingy open, a desk lamp with a swan-like neck craning over it. *So let's see how the corporate hot-shot makes his money*, I thought, and bent over the chart.

"At first I couldn't make it out. It didn't seem to be about business. There were several columns running across the page. In the left-hand margin, at the beginning of each column, was a woman's name: Jenny, Sue, Cindy, Jill etc. There were headings at the top of each column and that's when I started to feel short of breath and wobbly at the knees. The fifteen headings were: Face, Hair, Skin, Breasts, Waist, Arms, Legs, Privates, Feet, Backside, Scent, Adventurousness, Compliance, Availability, Confidentiality. There were percentage figures in each column beside each name and a final percentage total at the end. So take Cindy. She was high on most things, though a bit down on scent, and she bombed out on confidentiality. Poor girl! He thought she might blab. Look what she was missing out on! Poor bloody Jill – she bombed at both ends, face and privates. Thank God she had her tits going for her!

"Then came *the* moment! The last name on the list was mine: Solly! The spreadsheet to my right was virginal white. I wondered what I'd score when dick-head Robo-Lover assessed his night with me. But one thing was for sure – I wasn't hanging about to find out! I tiptoed back into the bedroom, got my gear on, and flew down the stairs, grabbing the muffins off the table as I went. *No way* was that jerk going to get my muffins! I got the key out from behind the statue and ran to the gate. I thought there'd be a button to press to open it but I couldn't see one and I was shit-scared that Robo-Lover would wake up and find me there. So I threw the muffins over the wall, climbed a lemon tree beside the gate, and lowered myself with a thump down the other side. When I phoned a taxi I was standing on one foot because *I'd wrecked my fucking ankle again!* But who *gives* a shit? I was outa there!"

My head pounding and lost for words, I feebly inquired, "And what happened to the muffins?"

"Well, they'd exploded into fragments in their bag when they hit the ground but they still tasted great, and *no way* was I going to sacrifice them because of *that fucker!* So I half-filled a bowl with muffin fragments, added soy milk and passionfruit yoghurt, a squeeze of lemon and had one of the best breakfasts of all time. All I can say is, thank goodness my gut instincts told me to get the hell out of there!"

"Sis," I said, "you're one shrewd and wise Solly."

"Yes" she replied, smiling like a schoolgirl on Prize Night, "you'd better believe it."

# Portrait of a Lady

After the death of his parents, Lionel Tremlett sold the family antiques business and purchased an apartment in a converted Tudor mansion high on a hill in Toorak. In warm weather he would sit reading and watching the Yarra River drift westwards below. In winter he read for long hours by the fire.

He took pleasure in pronouncing himself a "confirmed bachelor". He admired beautiful women, whom he saw as aesthetic objects, as portraits awaiting their painters, but had never been romantically drawn to one. Nor indeed to a man. His small group of friends liked to quote his genial self-characterization as a being "exempt from hormonal perturbation".

The cause of this exemption was unclear to him. His wintry and punitive Catholic childhood? But he didn't particularly care. Though often solitary, he was seldom lonely. Citing his beloved Henry James, he'd say that his life on the hill met "the requirements of my imagination".

At fifty he cut a casually refined figure: slim, upright, of medium height, his clean-shaven face unlined. He had straight dark hair, now threaded with grey, meticulously parted on the left side, and gentle chalk-blue eyes. In his customary grey slacks and tweed jacket, he would wander down to the faux Tudor shopping centre nearby, read the papers over coffee and pastry and attend to his emails. Then he would browse in a large, well-appointed bookshop.

The shop had been retitled "Mary's" when purchased some months earlier by a brother and sister. He had occasionally seen the brother, Martin, at the front counter, but never his sister, the eponymous Mary, who seemed to hover elsewhere like the Spirit of the Place.

This morning as he stepped into the shop's burnished interior – cream walls adorned by charcoal sketches of famous writers above polished wood shelves – he noticed a woman of middle age assisting an elderly customer. Something about her caught his eye and when she turned and looked in his direction, she was at once radiantly and sedately beautiful. She had shoulder-length dark, straight hair. Her white shirt was buttoned at the collar and beneath it a large turquoise and green pendant – the green repeated in her earrings – lay over the vee of a dove-grey chemise jumper. Her skirt and leggings were black, her low-heeled shoes a greyish green. Her red watchband echoed her lipstick. He was imagining her portrait when she walked over to him and asked in a mellifluous, slightly husky contralto whether she could be of assistance.

He stammered that he was looking for a recent biography of Edith Wharton.

"You're in luck," she said, drawing a hefty tome

down from a nearby shelf and handing it to him. "Are you a fan of hers?"

"I'm a particular fan of her friend Henry James and want to read more about their friendship," he stammered.

He turned the book over in his hands as a scholar might, opened it and ran his eye down the Table of Contents, thumbed through the glossy photographs in the middle, then checked the back cover's bio for the bona fides of the biographer. When he'd indicated his satisfaction with a sagacious nod, she gestured towards the counter and presently began to process the sale.

Unusually for him, he found himself watching her deft, slender hands for a glimpse of her ring finger. It remained hidden for a while behind a stack of books, then behind the cash register, then under the counter. At last it came into view. It bore a simple, thin, yellow-gold band. He watched intently as she slid the book and his receipt into a brown Mary's paper bag and taped it at the top. Smilingly, she held the parcel out to him and said, "Do come again."

"You can be sure I will," he replied. "I have long been a regular here."

\*

The ring's effect on him had been strange. He had hoped not to see evidence of her being attached, yet he was pleased to see that in all probability she was. Unavailable, this epiphanic being could remain a creature of the imagination. She had told him that they were short-staffed. She would work in the shop for the next six or so months. He began making daily visits. She always greeted him with a warm smile and gesture for him to wait while she served customers. Often, though, she was not there. When he inquired, staff said that she was "off-colour today", or that she was away visiting distributors.

One day, after a week's absence, she suggested morning tea at a cafe across the road. "So," she said when they had taken their seats at a table by the window, "I'm interested to hear what you made of the Wharton biography."

"I thought it was good," he replied, "and it helped to explain why the very private James was so taken with a woman who was so much out in the world."

"And what is your favourite James novel?" she asked.

"*The Ambassadors.*"

"I've never read it. Why that one?"

"Its main character, Strether," he replied, "is an enormously sophisticated man torn between engagement, being in amongst it, and living in his imagination. For me, he's the greatest character in literature. And your favourite novel?"

"I have two, *Anna Karenina* and *Madame Bovary.*"

"And why them?"

She paused, looked distractedly away, then said, "What the feminists call the shape of a woman's life, I suppose."

"I'm afraid I'm not au fait with feminism," he said.

"Probably just as well," she replied, getting up to return to the shop.

Over a few months, that epiphanic image of her began to colonize his thoughts.

At night he started doing something that he had not done since boyhood when his mother found him on his bed doing it, rushed out slamming the door, and told his father. "Don't you *ever* do that again!" the father had seethed.

Tremlett was feeling physically different. His hitherto languid body now felt taut, assertive, charged, sexual.

He did something else now for the first time. He imagined a woman naked. Mary would appear unexpectedly at his front door. While he was in the kitchen making coffee, she would disrobe in his living room and he would find her standing there, clothes diaphanous about her ankles like Aphrodite risen from the waves; her hair lapping delicate white shoulders, perfectly proportioned breasts, lips smiling gentle allure. He would follow her statuesque curves down to her flat stomach and to the perfectly manicured dark triangle, a faint hint of her womanhood curving between her thighs. Relishing his gaze, she would turn around for him to see her superb arched back and perfectly rounded buttocks. He would move towards her tense with desire … but the scene would stop there.

*

Her absences from work became more frequent. Sometimes when she returned she would look drained and distracted, but he was gratified that she still seemed pleased to see him.

They arranged lunch to "catch up" in a glass-walled deli across the road. They had been chatting for some time when her phone rang. She looked at it, dismissed the call and put it down again on the table. It immediately rang again, and again.

"You'll have to excuse me," she said and took the phone outside. Through the glass he could see her pacing about, gesticulating with her right hand, sometimes running it through her hair, speaking with some agitation. When she returned, he asked whether everything was alright.

"It's Walter, my husband. His sight is going. He's fallen at home and gashed a knee, poor darling."

"You go home and I'll take care of the bill," said Tremlett.

"No, I can stay. A neighbour is a retired nurse. I sent her a text. She'll dress the wound and calm him down. I don't want him to become too dependent on me."

"No, I suppose you have to keep an eye on the future."

"Well," she said, biting her lower lip and looking briefly away, "I don't imagine a future."

"You mean you can't imagine what it will be like?" he asked.

"No," she replied, "I don't imagine having one."

*

Tremlett pondered that conversation. "The shape of a

woman's life" could refer to the way these particular women's lives ended, or to the many and varied shapes women's lives could take. In any case, lots of readers would cite *Madam Bovary* and *Anna Karenina* as their favourite novels.

That odd comment about the future could be taken in various ways too. It might have been made in momentary despair after that upsetting call from her husband. Recently, in fact, she had been seeming quite jolly, as if a great weight had been lifted from her shoulders.

*

One evening the phone rang at 10:30. He did not recognize the number but sat up in bed to take the call.

"Hello, is that Mr Lionel Tremlett?"

"Yes, it is. Who's calling please?"

"This is Walter Fitzgerald. I think my wife Mary is a friend of yours?"

"Yes, indeed she is."

"Well," said Fitzgerald, "I am afraid there is very bad news."

He could hardly bear to hear what came next.

"I'm sorry to tell you that … Mary has had a complete nervous breakdown. She is in the psychiatric ward of St Peter's Hospital in a very bad state."

"I am most terribly sorry. I had no idea …"

"I have to tell you that she has been talking a lot about you. The staff have asked me whether the things she's been saying are true. Of course, I cannot say. She is severely, horribly confused. Would you mind my asking?"

"Of course not."

"She says that the two of you are lovers …"

"*My God!* No, this is absolutely untrue. There has never been even a hint of such a thing. We are friends. Not even particularly close friends."

"Thank you," said the husband. "I thought as much. She also insists that you were going to elope to Paris together. I now know this is absolute fantasy."

"Yes, completely and utterly. Has she been like this before?"

"Not this bad, but pretty bad. She has never got over her childhood. Her father was a monster. A pervert."

Fitzgerald now explained that Mary was refusing to cooperate unless she could see Tremlett and that the staff felt that a visit from him might be beneficial. The visit would have to be carefully supervised. He was to try, in neutral but kindly tones, to disabuse her of her delusions about him.

Next morning Tremlett took a lift to the floor of the psychiatric ward, followed signs through a maze of corridors, announced his arrival through an intercom and reported at the nurses' station. A nurse led him down the main corridor. People in pyjamas wandered distractedly along the grey carpeted aisle, some leaning against walls or talking animatedly to themselves. An elderly woman in a dressing-gown explained to the nurse that she had been a film star and cried, "Look how I've kept my looks!" In one of the rooms a man was shouting incoherently. In another a man was crying loudly, nurses trying to calm him. Life was "ferocious and sinister" – yes, James had said that too. Tremlett felt that the hubbub and the misery were raining down upon him. He walked with bowed head, attempting not to hear or see.

They reached the door of Mary's room. She was in bed, her back towards the door, knees pulled up. The nurse said quietly, "Mary, Mr Tremlett is here to see you," and backed out of the room to listen from the corridor.

Mary rolled over, looked at him and slid out of bed crying, "You're here. You're *here!*"

"Yes, Mary. It's good to see you. How are you?"

"Oh!" she cried, "*thank goodness!* No one would believe me. Can we go now?"

"Well …" stammered Tremlett.

"Yes, *of course* we can!" she said triumphantly, "and remember what is yours!"

She slipped her thick pink and yellow nighty down over her shoulders. It crumpled about her ankles. She stood naked before him.

It would be utterly wrong to look at her thus! Tremlett averted his gaze, but not before he had seen the unwashed dark hair hanging limply, wrinkles creeping down her graceful neck, her slanted shoulders drawing one breast higher than the other, a surgical scar under the left breast and another, lower down, disappearing into her thick bushy triangle from which isolated hairs straggled towards her slightly rounded abdomen. She spun gaily around, revealing dimpled buttocks and a large raised mole under her left shoulder blade. Somehow he had seen this too. Desperately he looked up into her face, searching for her above the excruciating humiliation of her nakedness. But this was not Mary. It was someone else altogether. Her lips were horribly contorted. Unseeing eyes stared at him through enormous pupils.

As he tried to unsee what he had seen, she rushed towards him and threw her arms around his neck sobbing, "Thank God you're here, thank God!" He stood rigid, but her aching misery went through him like a sword. He lifted his arms and rested each hand gently on her curved flanks.

The nurse rushed in. "What on earth is going on?! This will have to be reported!"

"She threw herself at me and I could not ignore her misery," he explained close to tears.

"Well, you'll have to go *immediately*," she said, dragging the now screaming woman from his arms.

As he made his way back down the hubbub of the corridor he could hear her wailing, "But he's my lover, my lover!"

*

He stepped into a small fluorescent-lit café on the ground level of the hospital. A bored-looking young woman chewing gum stood behind the cash register. A man in a dressing-gown sat in a corner doing a crossword puzzle. A couple in gloomy conversation sat near the door, one dabbing back tears. Tremlett ordered a coffee and sat down at a white plastic table looking out onto the street.

Two schoolboys walked laughingly by. An elderly woman, her husband beside her, made her laborious way with a walking frame towards the hospital door. A workman from a building site hurried in, ordered a Coke, sculled it, dumping the bottle in a trash can as he left. A truck juddered up to traffic lights opposite, spewing fumes as it lurched to a halt.

Lionel Tremlett saw it all with blinding clarity. The world outside was silent. He could hear nothing save the cries of that wretched creature upstairs, her face twisted in crazed misery, calling his name. He could not now imagine how, but he knew that when her mind was right again, the real Lionel Tremlett, whoever that was, would need to be there for her.

# Switzerland

They'd met at a symposium on the ethics of care and had been together, maintaining separate apartments, for two years before they married. She taught disability nursing; he was a professional ethicist, an advisor to government and private healthcare organizations. Her warm effusiveness and spontaneity were said to perfectly complement his polite sobriety. Even their looks were complementary: her long, expressive face framed by bobbing light-brown curls; his pale blue eyes peering benignly through frameless spectacles, thin black hair receding from his high, finely-lined forehead.

In their early forties when they met, each brought to their partnership sound professional reputations and disciplined work habits. The childless couple shared recreational interests: travel, the arts, bushwalking. Mutual moral admiration was fundamental to their bond. It was acknowledged between them that Penelope was "more the talker". James's self-containment sometimes left her lonely. He would indulge her need for connection until, nails digging into his palms, shoulders lifting slightly with tension, he would glaze over in a way calculated to call a halt. She never missed the signal. Yet she felt that, on the whole, they connected as well as most couples.

The bloom of romantic interest between them waned after the first year of marriage. She told herself it was always thus. And besides, theirs had never been a passionate physical bond. That was not what they had signed up for. There had been times, especially with her first boyfriend, when touch had a kind of fury, an annihilating power. But that was long ago, and she hadn't altogether liked it.

When the occasion arose, James was affectionately attentive to her needs, including her need for long, meandering conversations after they made love. Eventually she would doze tranquilly in his arms. Sometimes, thinking her too deeply asleep to notice, he'd ease himself out of bed, tiptoe to his study and work into the early hours. Always finely attuned to him, she'd sense his absence through the haze of sleep but remembered it, if at all, only vaguely in the morning.

He'd assure her that he wanted connection just as much as she but needed to feel that they could talk without "heavyosity", a neologism he quoted to their mutual amusement from Woody Allen. He wished, he said, "to enter a plea for conversation without complication".

After a while that signal became more peremptory. He was working incredibly hard. Penelope was a hard worker too but, she believed, in a rather different way. Her work did not seem to define her to the extent that his did him; but when she broached this thought with him, she got the familiar signal in short order.

*

An odd estrangement had insinuated itself into their bond. Even when they were together over a "relaxed" weekend she would feel on edge, even shy with him, as if marriage's expectation of intimacy had become an embarrassment. She wasn't sure that he felt this too, though she surmised from the chill of his forced jollity, and his shows of interest in her conversation, that he probably did.

She began to find a line from a poem running in her mind: "Nothing that is not there and the nothing that is." Was that how the line went? She'd studied the poem at school. A poem about cold and a snowman.

Curiously, some of their best moments now happened over the phone. She got into the habit of ringing him at his office around 11 a.m. when he'd break briefly for coffee and was feeling buoyed by work, before the fatigue that beset him later in the day had started to impinge. They'd catch up on work news, relax into marital banter, make plans for the coming weekend, holidays, a home renovation.

One morning he called before 11. There was a waver in his usually considered, fluent voice. Routine blood tests had come back with "a red flag of sorts". He had a rare but often treatable cancer that came in four strains. There were effective therapies for three of them. The fourth, however, was "more of a problem". He would have further tests to determine which strain it was and had an appointment with a specialist next week. If she wanted to "read up on the ague" in the meantime "that might be best". He'd "rather not".

She said reassuring things to make time for a quick scan of the Wikipedia entry as they spoke, and then said, "Well, you know, it's not what you want, but it sounds quite okay to me. There's only a 25 per cent chance you've got something that will be hard to treat and hard doesn't mean impossible. Also, of course, there'll be a lag time in the current information. Currently unpublished papers based on more recent research will describe new treatments and ones in the pipeline."

"Hmm …" he replied, and said no more.

Though mildly reassured by the snippets she'd given him, something like dread had settled in her soul.

*

If he was depressed or severely anxious during the days before the specialist's appointment, it didn't show. But once asleep in bed, he would hold her so tight that it hurt her ribs, and when he'd wake in fright in the early hours they'd talk until he was sleepy again, only occasionally referring to his illness.

The specialist's consulting room had a large window looking out onto a wide city street, sluggish with Melbourne trams trundling past lines of bare plane trees, and pedestrians swaddled against the cold. Penelope had an impression of an immaculately tidy white room, and noticed the dapper specialist's starched white collar and pastel grey tie that matched his eyes. James seemed dumb, almost absent.

As the doctor commenced his lengthy, carefully

modulated assessment, the trams and the cars outside started to blur before Penelope's eyes. Dull traffic noise would surge to a roar, then subside, ceding to the physician's discordantly calm voice.

She dared not look at James as the phrases fell from the specialist's lips: "The worst part of my job … nothing we can do for you except for palliation when the time comes … things you would really like to do … do them sooner rather than later. I'm sorry to be the bearer …"

James looked blank. Blank as they stumbled out into the greying dusk and onto a tram. When they reached Princes Bridge he made for the door. "I need to walk, walk, *walk!*"

They set off on a bitumen path beside the river, but soon he was bent over and shuffling, stopping every few steps until she had to hold him from falling. She helped him to a bench near the water's edge. The brown stagnant water gave off a faint, phosphorescent mist. The glowering sky found no reflection in the river's surface. On the path between the bench and the water, joggers in beanies puffed vapour as they pounded by. Walkers in anoraks, hoods up, meandered or strode, some with dog leads in gloved hands. A silence like a muffled howl entwined itself with the rumble of nearby traffic.

"So, what are you feeling?" she ventured.

"Nothing. I'm numb. Like a dead man walking. Which is what I am." And then, he bowed his head, face cupped in hands, elbows on knees, and wept uncontrollably. She drew an arm around him and wept with him, pressing her face against his. But he was rigid and unreachable.

Presently he stopped crying, sat up straight and seemed lost in thought for a very long time. And then he said, "I've got a plan."

"Yes …?"

"The doctor said to do stuff you've always wanted to do while there's time. So – I'll quit work and let's do that train journey through the Alps we've talked about. The one that starts in Munich, goes through Austria and ends in Zurich. We'll stay at a grand hotel on the lake before …"

"That's a wonderful idea," she sobbed.

"It'll be a 'destination holiday', but with one big difference."

"Yes …"

"I've read about a place outside Zurich by a lake that does assisted suicide for people from all over. After the train ride and a few days in a grand hotel, we'll proceed to the clinic and … I'll take matters into my own hands."

She paused as a wave of nausea swept over her. "*My God!* Are you *sure?!*"

"Yes, yes. If I've got to die early, I'm not doing it by shitty little degrees. The story ends my way."

Now followed days of travel bookings, coded farewells to relatives and friends, resignation letters, arrangements with the clinic on the lake. Penelope was astonished to find this usually sober man almost high on the "gig", as he called it, of orchestrating his own demise.

*

Three weeks later they were standing bleary-eyed in front of Munich's grand Gothic city hall. Next day they boarded a little red touring train with plush Victorian decor and glass-roofed observation cars. Legendary cities – Salzburg, Innsbruck, St Moritz, stunning in the glare of the blazing summer sky – flashed by or invited them in for sumptuous counterfeits of the sightseer's enchantment in cobbled streets, museums, opera houses, grand restaurants. Night stopovers were at chalets and fine hotels.

The train would chug to dizzying heights, bloom-dotted valleys shimmering in hyperreal perfection below, then loop down, hugging lakes and river banks, cruising past picture-perfect village hamlets. Everywhere gigantic peaks in the distance soared into azure blue.

Some days into the journey – they hardly knew how many – they alighted to view the Matterhorn. Leaning back and gazing through binoculars, James appeared transfixed.

"So what do you see?" Penelope asked.

"Nothing, really."

"What do you mean?"

"I mean, see where that cloud's wrapped around that snow-powdered peak?"

"Yes."

"There's nothing there. Blind, frozen nothing. They

call places like that death zones. You drown in your own lung fluid up there within minutes."

"Well," she said, brushing away tears, "some find it spiritual."

"No, there's *nothing* there. It's an upturned abyss. There's nothing spiritual in nothing."

Soon they were on their way again – Geneva, Interlaken …

*

When the two-week journey concluded, they booked into their turreted, pseudo-Gothic, wood-panelled hotel in Zurich overlooking the Limmat river. The aqua-blue waterway, girded by its magnificent architectural miscellany, sparkled and dappled with the vacant perfection of a postcard. The reflections of boats and pleasure craft rippled in the wakes they made.

It seemed extraordinarily odd that in the blazing heat of summer, the hotel kept a small, imitation gas fire going in one corner of the vast stone and timber entrance hall. But James liked it. He found the heat outside "merciless, annihilating"; but in front of the fire in a comfortable armchair, he felt "coddled", as if he were "curling up into a ball". So they agreed that in the mornings she would stroll the shops in the Bahnhoftrausse while he sat by the fire. They'd have lunch in one of the grand hotel dining rooms, rest, then read in the hotel library until dinner. On the seventh day they would attend their first appointment at the clinic and prepare for James's "next grand reservation", as he called it.

On the second morning of this arrangement, as she re-entered the hotel, Penelope saw two figures talking animatedly by the fire. She was surprised to find that one of these was James. When she walked over to them, James announced, "Jennifer, this is my wife Penelope. Penelope, meet Jennifer."

As the two women shook hands, the younger's light-green eyes sought contact with hers, apparently seeking approval for occupying her husband's time. She seemed to know what kind of time it was. Penelope smiled her approval, nodding slightly, as if to say she was fine with anything that might bring James a moment's solace. Jennifer, a slight woman of perhaps thirty, with straight blonde hair and a delicate pale complexion, eased relievedly back into her chair.

As they were making their way to their room a few minutes later, James explained that Jennifer was an art teacher in a school just outside London and was taking a few days' leave after the breakup of a long-term relationship.

"What sort of man would break up with a beautiful, sensitive young woman like *that?*" he asked. "Even now she has a kind of lightness, a natural solicitude, about her."

"Well, who knows? You can't see into other people's relationships."

The morning pattern continued for the next four days, except that when returning to the hotel, Penelope now used a side entrance to avoid disrupting the fireside conversation.

On the fifth day, James was not by the fire. He was in their room, curled up on the bed with a pillow perched over his eyes. He looked almost catatonic.

"What *happened?* Are you in pain? Did the situation …? Did you see Jennifer this morning?"

"Jennifer checked out early today. She had to get back to work."

"Would you like to talk about the situation? I feel we're going through this enormous thing together, but also strangely apart. Maybe, even this late, sharing can make a difference?"

"It might make a difference for you. I'll do my best. But honestly, for me what it is *is* what it is, and at least I know exactly where I stand."

She felt nauseous, vertiginous, even fleetingly angry, at this final rebuff; but in these last weeks the power of veto was absolutely, unarguably his.

*

He was still in this state when their taxi pulled up on an overcast day outside the clinic for their first appointment. The grey weatherboard premises resembled a modest two-storey Australian beach house. The small lake in the background looked torpid under the blanketing clouds.

The interior into which they stepped was similarly unprepossessing: faded prints of Alpine scenes hung on whitewashed walls; worn and rickety furniture. They were just announcing themselves to a woman in a white coat behind the reception desk when a tall, friendly-looking man emerged from an adjoining room, introduced himself as Dr Fritz Schweizer, and invited them in.

The solemnity they had expected was absent. Perhaps the doctor found these situations so confronting that he needed to feign good cheer?

He bid them to sit on a sofa and pulled up a chair in front of them. "So," he began, "you have come such a long way! A long, *long* way!"

"Indeed we have," said Penelope.

"So, my English is not very goot and I have something complicated to tell you. Not bad complicated. No, no. I think goot complicated. Yes, I definitely think so. Sometimes we go on a journey and it ends where we did not expect, no?"

He proceeded to explain that routine checks the clinic did with a "big tumour bank" in Philadelphia had just found a perfect match for James's case. The bank had reported "most excellent results" in treating this tumour with a "newly engineered" chemotherapy drug. Coincidentally, a Swiss research team had just been trialling a drug designed to block the flow of nutrients to a malignancy like James's. All with very encouraging results.

"I cannot promise anything. Cancer is so unpredictable. It does not obey rules. But, if you would like it, we can offer you a place in a trial here instead of what you have come for. We would give you the new treatments. If they do not work, we can then give you what you came for."

They asked what he thought the chances were. He repeated that he could not be sure but was "quite optimistic".

"If you were me, what would you do, Dr Schweizer?" asked James.

"I would have the trial. Yes. No doubt," replied the doctor. "You have nothing to lose, no? And if it works, you might have a long remission. Maybe even a long, long remission."

James agreed. They left the clinic in a state of numb delirium, hope vying with disbelief. He booked into the hospital. She took a room in a modest hotel nearby. Each day he'd receive his chemo through a drip as he lay in bed. When Penelope took breaks from his bedside, she'd wander through nearby galleries, shops and historic buildings.

Alone in his room, James started to write what he called the "Patient Journal: The medical ethicist gets his own medicine". He meant to closely monitor everything – the hospital ambience, the manner of the doctors and nurses, the way the vast contending forces of life and death, illness and flourishing, despair and hope, vied for sovereignty in this well-oiled anodyne institutional environment. He tried to track his own feelings as well, hour by hour, day by day, but he found this surprisingly hard to do.

*

Exhaustive tests were done after six weeks, and one morning Dr Schweizer came bustling into his room waving a fistful of charts. "I have *vonderful* news! The tests show remarkable tumour shrinkage. Yes. These are *amazing* results! And we think the tumour will not have enough nutrition to bounce back!"

The couple wept in one another's arms. Long-term chemo, the doctor explained, could be administered in Melbourne and elsewhere.

They checked in again to the grand hotel. This time they had a room with a balcony overlooking the Limmat river. They made love with an abandon they had never known.

On the first evening, they celebrated over a magnificent meal in the burnished wood-panelled hotel dining room. As they twined fingers across the table, James mused with mock solemnity, "We are here to give thanks; the only question is to what or to whom? To science, perhaps, or to dumb luck ..."

"Or," she interrupted, "to the Matterhorn peak?"

"Why that?"

"Because the deepest thanks need grandeur."

He looked quizzically at her, but said nothing.

For a few days they browsed the Bahnhoftrausse, toured museums and monuments. Once, in the entrance hall on the way out, Penelope pointed to the little fire and quipped, "Perhaps you'd rather be curled up like a ball in front of the fire?"

He smiled abstractedly and, taking her arm, drew her out into the street.

*

Back in Melbourne, it was agreed by all that the miraculous reprieve could not have happened to nicer people, to a more devoted couple, nor to people better equipped to navigate the vicissitudes of life-threatening illness. Each returned to work, but only on a part-time basis. They arranged their office hours to avoid too much overlap at home, to avoid "getting in one another's hair". In his spare time, James pressed ahead with the piece he had started writing in hospital. It had morphed from an observational memoir into a study of protocols of patient consent in the Swiss medical system.

Melbourne shimmered in the summer sun but James's mood cooled and so, Penelope felt, did the relationship. He was cut-off and preoccupied. It was like walking on egg shells. The old nothing – whatever that was – seemed to have taken up residence again between them.

"You seem awfully flat," she said one day.

"Do I?"

"Yes, you do, and I'm wondering whether you might have a touch of the remission blues – you know, where a reprieve brings an uncertain, open future, after the first burst of relief."

"I really don't think so," he replied. "I'm just happy to have the reprieve. I think I might've started working too hard too soon."

One day a few weeks later she came home earlier than usual. As she stepped from the glare into the cool shade of the hallway, she was surprised to hear his voice sounding animated and cheerful. Who was he on the phone to?

He was at the kitchen table, not on the phone, Skyping with someone on his laptop. As she drew near, she recognized the lanky blonde hair.

"Hi, honey. I'm just chatting with Jennifer. Remember her from the hotel?"

"Yes, I do indeed. Lovely to see you again, Jennifer."

At the bottom of the screen a time-elapsed digital clock was ticking over. Penelope saw that the couple had been talking for almost three hours.

She cooked dinner as usual and suggested a bottle of wine on the balcony. After the meal, as dusk descended, they moved to the living-room sofa, glasses in hand.

"So," she began, "you and Jennifer seem to have struck up quite a friendship."

"Well, she's a nice young woman and I enjoy her company."

"Is that all?"

"What do you mean?"

"I mean, you'd been talking for almost three hours today and I assume you talk fairly often?"

"Well, yes, but I don't attach any great significance to that."

"The reason you don't attach any great significance to that is that you're a stranger to your own unconscious."

"What *on earth* does *that* mean?!"

"Never mind. That's for another conversation. Another day. What I really want to say is that we've come through this amazing experience together but we're back to where we were. There's a sort of nothing between us. We're close friends but something is still missing. We've come through the flames but there are ashes between us. We need to make a change. A big one."

He looked shocked, almost shattered. She wanted to lean over and put an arm around him to comfort him. But she didn't.

She pressed on, momentarily softening her tone. "One thing we do know is that you're a dab hand at travel arrangements ..."

"Sorry?"

"Another thing it seems to me that we know," she said with cool deliberation, "is that Jennifer offers you something that I can't, and that you need."

"That's *absurd!* I hardly know her. I'm fifteen years older than her. She's just a warm, uncomplicated presence at a complicated time."

She looked at him with pitying resentment and incredulity but said nothing more. It began to dawn on him how utterly her mind was made up, how icy was her resolve.

*

Three days later she moved into an apartment with sweeping views of Port Phillip Bay.

A month after that he was on a plane to London.

# High Noon at Starbucks

One blazing day soon after we got to Florida, I set out for Highlight Reel Sports, a second-hand sports store next to the local Starbucks. It was a great barn of a place with a thundering air-conditioning system: the arctic blast – a welcome change from the tropical furnace outside – came laced with the odour of pre-loved sports gear. Back home, I'd often loitered in sports stores like this, miming a serve with a graphite tennis racquet, tossing a glossy cricket ball, or hand-balling a pristine Sherrin to myself.

But here, everything was alien: baseball bats in serried ranks, gridiron helmets and protective padding, scarred basketballs, footwear that bore no relation to any sport I'd seen. So I was relieved to discover familiar tackle in one corner: golf clubs. My game. My favoured kind of club had been a "hybrid", so-called because its shape combines blade iron and driver. And the first clubs I saw in Highlight Reel Sports were hybrid irons. Cleveland too – a reputable brand!

I went up to the guy behind the counter, a colossus, well over six feet, a veritable slab of a man. His sandy wavy hair was roughly parted above a broad red face criss-crossed with delicate capillaries and dotted with sun-spots. Varicose veins snaked from his tree-trunk-like thighs down to sandaled feet, traversing knees striated by long shiny-white surgical scars. The slab of him fanned out at the knees, so bowed that there was room enough for a basketball between them.

I asked about the clubs. Were they any good? Sure, he told me. "Highlight Reel Sports does not sell garbage, sir. Cleveland's a great brand." Could I try them out? Sure I could. Buy them, road-test them at the range, and get a full refund if not satisfied – provided they came back within three days.

He paused.

"You from Australia?"

"Yes," I said. "You've picked the accent straight off."

"I was there about ten years ago with a school basketball team. It's one helluva place!"

"True. What parts did you visit?"

"We started up in Queensland. Very like Florida. Then we went down to Sydney. Stayed near Kings Cross. Now there's a place! Holy shit! I've never seen anything like it! There were hookers on every corner. There was a big college just nearby and a lot of the hookers were students. You couldn't walk a block without getting the eye and some of those gals were somethin' else!"

"How did you know they were students?"

"Everyone said they were. You could see it. You could see their nipples through their t-shirts. They weren't your usual hooker."

"The Whore of Mensa" came to mind but I refrained from that allusion.

"So, where did you go after Sydney?"

"We took the team to Canberra, to a place called the Institute of Sport. We played a game there against some kids from 'round the country."

"And how did that go?"

"Well, we lost the game but we won the fight. There was a huge brawl. Kids on the floor throwing punches. We had to get in and break it up. Security guards came running in and it was on the front page of the paper next day!"

"Jeez," I said, "what a disaster!"

"Nope. When you're a small school, all publicity's good publicity."

I paid for the clubs and a bag, saying that I hoped not to see him again, "because, sir," I hastened to add, "it would mean that I liked the clubs."

\*

I'd sold our little publishing business in Melbourne and was about to retire there when my wife was offered a job in northern Florida. What better place to retire than northern Florida? We were to live in Port Glades, one of the wealthiest postcodes in the country and a retirement Mecca, a place where people really knew how to retire, to kick back, slow right down, laze in the sun, roam the area's innumerable golf courses, and socialize in its oak-lined club houses.

I am a sociable man. People in the estate were fast with friendly greetings. But that seemed to be about it. I'd never known anything like this climate's power of penetrative enervation. I'd generally venture outdoors in the afternoon when the blaze had gone off the day and the alligators which flourished in the nearby ponds came out to predate. Route A4A, the provincial highway that ran past the manicured grounds of our gated community, had no public transport, and I had no car. An imitation Gilded Age bicycle came with our rented house, but its seat was too high and I had no tools to adjust it. The house was large, luxurious and would have been just right for a family. My wife worked a sixty-hour week, so it was just me during waking hours, shifting camp from room to room. I'd never done solitude well. I was a nervous wreck in Nirvana.

Once I had my set of Clevelands I joined the golf club. Well within walking distance, it was the hub of social life. Before my first round, I thought I'd break the ice with a beer in the clubhouse. I ordered a Samuel Adams at the bar, and said, "Hi" to the prosperous-looking, white-haired, tanned guy in a shiny blue golf shirt on the stool to my right.

"Well, Ah'll *be*. You're Australian? Ah've never bin there. But I guess you have?"

"You guessed right, sir!" I said, sucking at my beer. "I'm Nathan."

"Well, Nathan, mah name's Jim. Ah ran mah own automobile business in Georgia for forty years then moved here to reward mahself. Mah first wife, Jen, was a great gal, but she died of cancer. Now mah second wife, Suzie, she's doing a great job for me."

*

This good news lifted my spirits like a traffic infringement notice.

I began to acculturate. There was a television in virtually every room of the house, including the bathrooms, and a gigantic one in the living room which doubled in mysterious ways as a radio. My wife showed me how to access theme radio stations which ran on a sort of endless loop, 24/7. One of these was the Frank Sinatra station which in fact only played a Sinatra number every six or so songs but had the virtue of inviting comparison between Sinatra and other crooners. Indeed Ol' Blue Eyes towered over his contemporaries, but why? What was so different? And didn't he often sing flat? These questions began to colonize my mind. I'd track them on Google during the day and would re-hash them with my wife when she got home from her twelve-hour working days.

"You know," I tried to explain, "Sinatra really is head and shoulders above the other crooners, but I can't figure out why. His voice has a big turning circle, like an old American car."

She listened patiently, if abstractedly, for several evenings but then came clean. "I really don't care. I've never liked him. And he was a thug anyway."

"Well yes," I replied, seizing on what looked like an opening for more analysis, "but part of his cultural fascination is how a great artist – and he *does* seem to have been that – can be so beholden to the mob. Family and friends say the links weren't deep, that the mob owned a lot of the places where those singers had to perform. Mia Farrow was married to him. She defends him over that. But then she says that when Woody Allen eloped with one of her adopted daughters, Sinatra offered to have the mob break both his legs."

"A pity they didn't," she said. "So, how are you feeling?"

"As flat as a night carter's hat," I replied, smiling wanly at the laconic inventiveness of that arcane Aussie locution.

"I'm just trying to be sympathetic," she said.

*

The best company in the vicinity was a group of retirees, drop-outs and drop-ins who gathered each day at the Starbucks. They'd spend hours in the U-shaped configuration of armchairs and sofas at the front of the establishment. It being the summer vacation, most of the staff were college and high school kids. Behind the service desk was a sliding window for the drive-through section.

Once I'd seen a sheriff's car pull up there; it had "SHERIFF: PSA" emblazoned on each side window. I emailed my prostate cancer specialist in Melbourne, joshing that the authorities here seemed to police prostate cancer tests like nowhere else. It turned out that this PSA stood for Public Service Assistant, a junior law enforcement position.

This was northern Florida, a Republican stronghold with a church on every corner. I kept bumping into seemingly normal people who were intending to vote for Trump. The Starbucks regulars included Frank, a retired Baptist minister. Short and rotund, he had glossy brown hair that belied his age, and good-humoured blue eyes behind surprisingly garish red-framed glasses. He was a more sympathetic man than his conservative pronouncements might suggest.

So was Molly, a warm woman, perhaps in her seventies, a mother of three who had worked in real estate. Carefully attired, her slightly unruly grey hair and pinkish complexion gave the impression that she had dozed off under her hair drier. She didn't seem shy but didn't say a lot, apparently preferring to listen. She had an odd habit of turning her head down and to one side, withdrawing her eyes from her surroundings, and laughing quite heartily to herself, her round tummy wobbling, often for no discernible reason.

Then there was Max, an old businessman with a multi-coloured cane, a deep rasping voice, thin wisps of white hair and a sun-battered red complexion. He acted the curmudgeon but was gruffly companionable, funny and loved to bait people with outrageous right-wing claims.

And Bob, a short, plump feisty man whose red baseball cap proclaimed: TRUMP: MAKE AMERICA GREAT AGAIN. His steel rim glasses steamed up when the talk got political, as it often did.

I'd pop in for an hour or so. After witnessing The Discourse of the Starbucks Right, the world would never be the same. One of the occasional drop-ins who worked as a medical aide believed that Michelle Obama was a transsexual. No photos of her and her children had ever been seen, he contended, in which the youngest daughter was less than four years of age.

Another, a fireman who delivered furniture on weekends to make extra cash, said when I asked him how he might vote, "Well, Ah'm old school, like mah Dad. Ah work hard. Real hard. And Ah don't see whyAh have to pay taxes to keep people who have killed other folk alive in prison. Ah don't really follow politics, but Ah just have a feelin' Trump would be the kinda guy who'd do something 'bout that. Ah mean, if there's any doubt whether someone killed someone else, you wouldn't kill them. But when you know for sure that they did it, Ah say do the same to him so mah taxes don't go to keeping him alive in prison for the rest of his life."

A couple of aged armed services veterans completed the cohort of regular Right attendees.

The less populous Left was spearheaded by the articulate, bombastic Ron, a retired lawyer who taught the Constitution at a local community college, knew his American history, and was exempt from doubt about anything. He'd lean forward in his fraying collarless t-shirt, ample belly spilling over on to his running shorts, and give it to the Right with both barrels, his baseball cap bobbing in time to the drubbing. He would grill them, demand to know what exactly they had just said had to do with anything, tell them what was "actually" in the Constitution, and denounce them as "knuckleheads", "Bible-bashing slow learners", and so on. When the others saw him coming they'd groan, "*here he comes!*"; yet they seemed actually to enjoy his company.

Conjoined by loneliness, distaste for the costly, opulent, "snowbird" culture across the highway, and the appeal of one another's craggy eccentricities, the group rumbled on until the morning after the election. An occasional visitor, a committed Trumpian, dropped by to share the result with Ron. So heated was the sharing that they adjourned to the car park to settle things by fist. Ron spent the evening in the county jail and was permanently banned from Starbucks.

It was harder to read Warren, the other mainstay of the Left. Straight long white hair brushed back, t-shirts cut off at the shoulders, jeans and a grizzled grey-blue-eyed face, he might have been a retired Pro Wrestler in miniature. He'd run a successful plumbing business and, when in the mood, was the most reflective of the group. But his mood bounced about from day to day, and on a bad one he could be silent or monosyllabic for hours.

The first time I met him a fine Sinatra rendition of "Autumn Leaves" had just begun on the café's music loop. I ventured, "Are you a Sinatra fan?"

"No. Never liked him. Overrated."

I tried another tack: "I see you here a lot. Seems like this is your office?"

"Living room, more like it."

One day I arrived early, with the pooch, and ordered a bagel and Perrier water. The young woman at the cash register had glossy black hair that cascaded over her shoulders but was crowned by a grove of vertical spikes. She glared at me with her deep-brown eyes. What was my crime? Welshed on coffee, Starbucks's stock-in-trade? Stared at her ear and nose studs? Being a man? A man aged sixty-five?

Right and Left were already hard at it. Anthony Wiener, a sometime Democrat Congressman, and his wife, Huma Adebdin, a senior aide to Hilary Clinton, had just announced their separation. Weiner had already been in trouble for sexting photos of his private parts to women who were not his wife. He had been at it again. But this time he'd sunk to a new low: he'd taken a selfie, in his customary state of arousal, albeit on this occasion in his briefs, with their young son next to him in the frame, and sent it to a lady Trump supporter. Bob was inclined to see all of this as a reflection of the moral iniquity of the Clinton campaign. Ron was having none of it.

Ron: "It's got *nothing to do with the Clinton campaign!* The man is a creep, a jerk! That's all!"

Bob: "Well, I think it does have something to do with it. Abedin's mother believes in Sharia Law."

"So what!" exploded his now scarlet interlocutor. "*So what!* All sorts of people in this country believe in all sorts of things but that doesn't mean they become law. Congress makes the laws and it's not about to enshrine Sharia Law for the American public. Just *read the Constitution, knucklehead!*"

Bob took a tug at the peak of his MAGA cap and considered his next move. I looked across at Warren. He was absolutely fuming, eyes narrowed, shaking his head slowly in disbelief.

Just then Mr Colossus from Highlight Reel Sports strode in.

"Not *him!*" snarled Warren.

The colossus paused, looked at me, and announced, "Hey! Here's my Australian buddy!"

He turned to the rest. "I was just telling this guy the other day about when me and the team stayed near King's Cross and there were these hookers on every corner, and a lot of them were college students. There was a big college just nearby."

Warren struggled to his feet, threw his iPhone onto his armchair, and shouted, "What would you know, you big lunk? If I hear that story one more time I'll take you out with one of your fucking baseball bats! How would you know whether a prostitute was a college student or not? You wouldn't have a clue!"

"Everybody knew. You haven't been there. And besides, the regular ones dressed up more. The college girls wore t-shirts with no bra so you could see their nipples standing out."

Now the temperature went up a notch. Warren launched himself arthritically at the man-monolith who was about to throttle him.

I considered thrusting myself into the fray to restore

order. But I'm a coward and the dog was yapping hysterically. Then something happened that rendered intervention unnecessary.

The young woman who had served me jumped out from behind the counter and addressed the assembled clientele at the top of her lungs: "You pathetic meat-heads! Is it any wonder we've got a sociopath running for President!? This testosterone-driven culture isn't fit for a dog! Just look at you! – a pair of grown men arguing about whether college students are hookers and have their nipples poking through t-shirts! What would a pair of sexist losers like you know anyway? Well, I'm a college student and I can tell you – I don't earn extra cash on street corners! I earn it *here*, serving dinosaur fucking fossils like you! But if you want college student nipples, *I'll show you nipples!*"

And with that she flung off her Starbucks apron and black t-shirt, unhooked her bra and stood, pink nipples pert in the refrigerated air, glowering at the silent combatants.

*

Now a PSA sheriff's car pulled in at the take-out point and the kid manning the window shouted, "'Scuse me, officer, but we seem to have a public affray in here. Better get in here quick!"

A minute later a police officer rushed in, took one look at the girl and yelled, "What the?! You're coming with me, young lady!"

He wrapped his jacket around her shoulders and bundled her out the door.

There was another passage of dead air. Bob shook his head in appalled disapproval, but clearly felt called upon to witness the outrage unfolding before him.

I found myself rather taken with those nipples and reflected that I would need to describe the incident with some care when recounting it to my wife.

Eventually Max broke the ice: "Well, that's the best thing that's happened to my hormones in decades. That young lady just restored my faith in American youth!"

Frank chuckled. "Ah thought Ah'd seen everything in forty-five years in thah ministry, but apparently *not!*"

Molly sat, head averted, eyes almost closed, her round belly undulating with silent laughter.

*

A few weeks later I asked the kid who'd urged the police to intervene what had happened to the girl who'd been taken into custody.

"Not much," he said. "She's the sheriff's daughter."

# The Patient

(After Herman Melville's *Bartleby the Scrivener*)

Though I am a doctor, I myself am not entirely well. I like to help and like to think that I do at least sometimes help, dispensing such comforts, cures and stays against calamity as I can from my little GP's two-man practice in Malvern.

Sometimes, once or twice a year, I feel a change coming. It usually starts with a dream. I'm trudging down a dirt road in blazing heat. The sky darkens to a huge ragged beaked shadow. Great oily rustling black wings feather my shoulders and close about my head. I'm flung up and up and up ... and then dumped, plummeting ... I wake startled, glazed in perspiration, gripped in panic. Putrid gloom starts to ooze through my veins.

I ring my partner and say I'll need a week off for rest and fine-tuning of my medication. He understands. For want of a better name we call this malady, which sent me packing from a childless marriage a decade ago, depression.

*

Our PA, Pam, is the very soul of discretion. An extraordinary array of people pass through a GP's waiting room – the whole gamut of human pain, need and peculiarity – but not once have I seen Pam extend anything less than respectful calm even to the most difficult patients. Her parted short ginger hair frames a kind face, and her light-blue eyes exude welcoming reassurance.

But this day when I stepped out of my consulting room to usher in my next patient, she looked troubled and, passing me the clipboard bearing the first-appointment questionnaire, said, "We have a new patient today, Dr Simms. Mr Emmett says that he would rather convey his personal information to you in person."

I looked down at the patient information form and indeed, aside from the name Bartle Emmett, written in a curiously inconsistent hand – now slanting this way, now that – nothing was to be gleaned. Even such routine questions as Date of Birth, Address, Marital Status, met the response, "TBA" – to be advised. This was a first.

I conducted him into my room and gestured towards a chair to the right of and facing my own, my custom being to sit behind my desk and swivel to face my patient. Seeing that he seemed bemused – or perhaps apprehensive – about this, I said, "So, Mr Emmett, what brings you here today?"

"I do not like doctors and I do not often see one."

He spoke with slow, almost robotic, deliberation and he had an unusual habit of swallowing saliva between clusters of words, so that his thoughts were punctuated by a gulping sound, *gng*, like the warble of a song bird.

I took a couple more paces towards my desk and turned to face him. He was a shortish thin man of perhaps early middle age. His dark hair was parted on one side but cut so high off his ears that the hair below the parting jutted out in a little wedge. His facial hair left a dark shadow where he had deployed his razor to good effect, but thin lines of stubble high on his cheek bones marked a point beyond which that implement had ceased to avail. His chin was specked with stubble. He wore thick black plastic-framed glasses, one arm of which had been secured by a vertical sliver of silver duct tape. My attempt at eye contact was thwarted by a certain untrusting reserve in him, and also by his eyes: he had a "lazy" left eye, the pupil fringed by red veins, hooded by an uncommonly low eyelid, which pointed slightly to the left and up as the other looked straight ahead. He wore a nondescript white shirt, a loose-fitting faded blue jacket, and dark blue trousers that hung centimetres above dusty black shoes. I noted with guiltily mounting distaste that his unusual salivary habits left little drifts of froth in the corners of his lips. I could sense nothing, not even the merest hint of energy or sociability, in his strange aura.

Having absent-mindedly lowered himself into the chair, he said, "Do not conclude, please, that because I have come to see you today I will come again. It is my hope and expectation that only one appointment will be necessary."

I explained a little curtly that I could not give him assurances on this point and that doctors have to base their recommendations on assessments of their patients' health.

If this made any impression on him it was not obvious to me. One eye looked straight past me, the other off and away. His face was immobile. After a long pause, he suddenly announced, "It is possible, I believe, that I may have a depression."

I could feel my psychic defences creaking into place, an emotional drawbridge making ready to rise. But seldom had I seen a soul so forlorn. I found myself telling him, rather to my surprise, "I myself am no stranger to depression. In fact, I know it all too well."

He received this with complete impassivity. He continued to stare past me, apparently pondering, and then replied, "I am not used to the way you doctors talk and I do not like it. What is it that you can do for me?"

My attempt to make connection seemed to have vanished into a vast darkness that now surrounded him, a black halo silhouetting his head. I felt myself drifting as if bleeding beyond my own outline.

Another long pause and then, looking quite intently at me with his level eye, he asked, "Have you ever been evicted from your home?"

"No," I stammered. "Have you?"

"Yes, that is what happened to me. That is when I started to feel, perhaps, *gng*, depressed."

Now at last he surrendered up a few fragments of his life-story. He had modest "independent means", had never worked; he did not wish to discuss his earlier life; did not want me to make inquiries about him. Three years ago, he had been forced out of his home; and for those three years, indeed a little longer than that since he had received prior warning of this upheaval, he had been experiencing a feeling that he called "depression".

"For many years I rented a little house, *gng*, in Surrey Hills. It was just an old little wooden house with peeling paint, *gng*, tattered carpets and dingy rooms. It had been rented for me by my uncle when my mother died, *gng*, and the rent was paid each month by the bank. He's dead now and I never knew who owned the house, *gng*. But it was *my* house. Then a letter came. I would have to find another place to live because my house was going to be knocked down. I lay in bed for many days and then a lady – a social worker – came to see me. She said nothing could be done. I would have to find another house. She would help me. Now I live in Richmond. But I was evicted, *gng*, from my house.

"I knew when my house was supposed to be knocked down. I got the train to Surrey Hills to see if it would really happen. A man came with a huge truck and a big tractor-like contraption on the back that had a gigantic iron shield at the front. I said to him, *gng*: 'What are you going to do?' He said 'I'm going to demolish the fucking house, mate. What do you reckon?' I didn't say anything. I thought it would take a long time to do that job. I didn't want to watch but I could not leave. I thought *I'll just watch today*. I thought it would take several days. But the man just drove that thing off the back of the truck, pointed it at my house and drove straight through it. In a few minutes the house was, *gng*, in pieces, great clouds of dust swirling off of it. I could not believe it. I got the train back to Richmond and lay down again for many days. I wanted to feel nothing again, but, *gng*, I could not."

The paralysing power of his colossal, uncomprehending gloom almost struck me dumb; but he had at least given something of himself, and I needed to speak. I mentioned post-traumatic stress syndrome as a possible source of his depression. But he did not want labels. He wanted pills.

"I am told there are pills for depression called Prozac. I would like you please to give me some of these. If you do, I will come back in three days to tell you whether they are working. Otherwise this will be our only appointment."

I explained that I did not yet know enough of him to prescribe a powerful medication, and that anyway it would take at least three weeks for Prozac to work, if it was going to.

This made no impression on him and he leant forward, his hands on the arms of the chair, as if to get up and leave.

Desperate, I tried another tack. I could organize for him to have eight subsidised appointments with a psychologist who would make an informed assessment of his depression and recommend the best way forward.

"No," he said, "I prefer not to see a psychologist,"

and he looked away so hard, I knew he was having none of it.

"Very well then," he announced, "that is the end of our first and only appointment," whereupon he raised himself with surprising dexterity from the chair and stalked towards the door.

He let himself out before I could get to the door. I resumed my seat and found that two feelings were contending for my soul. I wanted him to go. I did not want him to go.

I was upbraiding myself for failing so abjectly with such a wretched patient when a text message from Pam arrived: "cld u plse see Mr Emmett out asap!!" I hastened to the reception area where I found her leaning as far back as the wall behind her desk chair would allow and Bartle Emmett, bent at the waist like a stick figure, leaning towards her over the desk, apparently trying to make conversation. The alarmed Pam gestured with her eyes towards the front door whence I escorted Mr Emmett with a firm arm around his bony back, stepped out onto the path outside with him and bade him a gruff farewell.

"What on earth *happened?*"

"It's hard to say," said Pam, "but I do not feel safe with that man. He seemed to have no idea about paying an account – maybe he was pretending about that, I don't know – but he started ogling me over the desk and asking me questions."

"Such as?"

"He asked whether I had a family and a family

home and how long we had lived in it. When I said yes and twenty years he asked about my husband. He kept making strange gulping noises every few words."

"Hell!" I exclaimed. "I'm very sorry, Pam. *My God!*" I shot back into my consulting room.

*

I phoned Graham, a psychiatrist and old medical school friend. He'd been a great support over the years, talking me through my terrible lows, the marriage breakup, managing my medication. He'd often urged me to see a psychiatrist on a "proper professional footing" – "therapeutic friendship has its limits," he would say. But somehow I'd never got around to it.

We agreed to meet at a café and I pulled up two chairs beside a huge window that looked out onto Burke Road, Camberwell. A fierce summer northerly was tossing swirling leaves and debris about under a glowering grey sky. A sheet of newspaper lifted and flapped into the bull bar of a tram as it chugged uphill into the wind. Presently Graham came through the tumult, his abundant white hair dishevelled, tie loosened and blue coat collar turned up as if against the cold.

We ordered coffee. He leant his arms on the table, his kindly grey eyes looking straight into mine. "So … your patient …"

Immediately it spilled out of me – Emmett's woebegone appearance, his guttural tic, his entropic aura. I said that he appeared to lack a wavelength for human connection and described the scene at Pam's desk. Might he, I asked, be a danger to women? Could he be suffering from PTSD? I explained what I had recommended to him and that he had refused to see a psychologist. I doubted that he would return to my rooms, but what should I do if he did?

"So, as to women," Graham began, "I don't know. You say he has reached perhaps early middle age. It might be wise to make inquiries with the police. Certainly don't leave him alone with Pam. But my guess is that he's probably sexually quiescent. PTSD? Perhaps, particularly if there had been early neglect or abuse. The missing wavelength might suggest a psychotic illness or autism. Depression? Not in any simple sense."

"It certainly feels like depression," I said.

"Well, okay," he said, "but what I really want to say to you" – and here his eyes hardened – "is that it would be a big mistake for you to become entangled with a man like that. I know you want to help. You always do. But all you're likely to do is drag yourself down. Your own depressive tendencies leave you wide open. You've given him the right advice."

"Yes," I said, "I know you're right." And I meant it.

*

I heard nothing from Emmett but he was constantly on my mind. I'd often ask Pam whether there had been any sign from him. He'd become a sort of haunting. I'd picture him in the chair beside my desk, impassive as stone, sometimes silhouetted in his dark halo, or his head dissolving into a flock of birds like a vector diagram.

Then several weeks later he appeared unannounced at my rooms. It was during lunch, so Pam was out. I felt the strangest mix of dread and jubilation.

"How have you been these past weeks?"

He said there had been no change and that he still wanted me to give him Prozac. I repeated that I could not, at least until I had a better idea of what was causing his depression. I again suggested seeing a psychologist. He repeated – this time with tart irritability – that he preferred not to. He then returned to the subject of his eviction, which he apparently saw as the cause of all his ills.

He now lived in a one-bedroom flat.

"Are you comfortable there?" I asked.

"I do not wish to be comfortable there," he replied. "It is not my home."

He had a strangely disorienting effect on me. I had not written him a script, but we seemed to have embarked on the rudiments of a conversation. No, I would not get "entangled" with this man, but I would do what I could while I could, and then firmly leave off. So I said, "This may surprise you, Bartle, but I have a consuming passion – one that has nothing to do with my work. It is test cricket. In fact, I plan my annual leave so that I can see every ball bowled at the MCG in the Boxing Day Test. Do you have such a passion?"

He paused and then said, "Solitaire."

"You enjoy solitaire?"

"I play solitaire on my computer. I play for many hours at a time. Sometimes at a café. I play and play and play until I feel nothing. This is what is agreeable to me. When the last cards go flying home like little birds to a nest, this is agreeable also."

Lunch break was just ending and I explained that I had to see other patients now. Again he seemed to ponder, lost in some vast inner silence. As I saw him off at the path he surprised me by holding out a hesitating hand. I took his in mine and enfolded my other hand firmly about his extended wrist. He said nothing and presently wandered away down the thronged suburban street.

*

Now another long silence from Bartle. Again, I wanted and did not want to see him.

One day Pam put a call through to me from a woman who said she wanted to talk to me about Mr Bartle Emmett. My heart began to race as the voice on the other end said, "Hello, doctor. My name is Suzanne. We have a gentleman here by the name of Bartle Emmett who says he is a patient of yours. We have asked him to leave but he seems rather confused. He says he doesn't have a family so I am ringing you."

*It would be a big mistake for you to become entangled with a man like that* … How well I knew it, and how powerless I was to abide!

"Thank you for contacting me, Suzanne. I am indeed Mr Emmett's doctor and I would be pleased to take responsibility for him on this occasion. Please give me your address and I will come straight over."

I could barely drive for agitation but eventually arrived at a large old terrace house in Richmond, its faded wrought iron balustrading threading its way across high windows, each blanketed by heavy burgundy curtains. To my surprise the front door was locked and was further secured by a large padlock and chain. A sign to the right advised "clients" to use an entrance off a little laneway. I made my way along parched pavement, casting a shadow that did not look like mine. I came to another sign: *Suzanne's – Women of Leisure for Men of Action* and it dawned on me what manner of establishment this was! After announcing myself on the intercom, a tall stilettoed woman of middle age in a charcoal-grey pinstriped suit unlocked the door, let me in, offered her hand and said, "Suzanne". She gestured across the faded ornate entrance hall, overhung by a massive chandelier, to a black and white striped chaise longue in a corner. There sat a scantily-clad young woman apparently in earnest conversation with Bartle Emmett.

"Good God!" I blurted. "Does he come here often?"

"We've never seen him before. He just seems to want to talk. Lots of men wander in here for company, some warmth from a woman. For a guy like this, sex isn't even on the radar."

"So you don't think he could be some kind of sexual deviant, a danger to women perhaps?"

"No, he's harmless. He just wants his mother."

As I approached I saw that Emmett sat turned and leaning in towards the young woman. Her right hand conveyed gentle restraint on his left shoulder, but she did not seem to be shrinking from him. Perhaps I imagined it, but the white saliva drifts at his lips' edge were even more prominent than usual.

She gave me a knowing smile and, if I am not mistaken, a sly grin seemed to flit momentarily across his face as well. Whether or no, he was soon his old impassive self again, and after some strong encouragement from me, seconded by the ladies, my patient and I stepped out into the laneway.

"Bartle, what *on earth* were you doing in a place like *that*?"

"I believe," said he, "that I had an agreeable visit. The ladies were pleased to see me."

The conversation now skipped about almost playfully – indeed, I had never seen my "patient" so cheerful – until I had escorted the unsuspecting Lothario to my car. Now, for the first time in all my dealings with him, I really laid down the law.

"Bartle, I am going to drive you home. I am going to come in with you for one last chat. This time *no argument please*. This is just the way it is!"

To my surprise he acceded without the slightest resistance.

*

His flat was on the third floor of a cream brick building common in the sixties. He led me up worn carpeted stairs and opened the door onto a living area – soiled white walls, a faded floral rug, and a glass light fitting an inch deep in dead insects. There wasn't a stick of furniture in the sitting area, but beside the bench that separated kitchen and "living room" stood a straight-backed dark wooden chair and a small wood-laminate table. Upon the latter sat a laptop and a packet of corn-flakes. On an orange Laminex counter beside the stove were a toaster, frying pan, electric kettle and three pieces of cutlery. At the base of a wall lay a mattress with pillow and blanket.

"Is this where you sleep, Bartle?"

He nodded assent and then stood impassive.

"May I see the other rooms?" I asked, gesturing towards a short passageway.

Again, he nodded.

Behind the first door was the toilet. The second, which reeked of mouldy dust, was crammed almost to the ceiling with old furniture – threadbare floral armchairs and a matching sofa, an upturned table, knick-knacks, a framed print of *Leda and the Swan*, books and papers flung about. Many of the smaller items were piled on a wire bed base. A mattress, its stuffing disgorging through rent fabric, rested upright against a wall. I closed the door and returned to the living area.

"Bartle," I said, "there is a bed in there. Why don't you use it? And comfortable chairs …"

"I find my corner, *gng*, cosy. It is my lair," he said, seeming faintly amused at his own choice of word. "Perhaps the doctor would like to sit down?" he said, turning his head towards the chair.

I was feeling foggy, faintly nauseous. That mattress and the thought of annulling sleep was almost appealing. I lowered myself into his wooden castaway. He remained standing by the stove, jacket and trousers hanging as if from a scarecrow, looking down at, past and through me in one act of entropic inattention.

"Well, Bartle, you have indeed managed not to establish a new home for yourself," I said.

Perhaps in the fragile arc of this life, eviction was a unique catastrophe. Perhaps he had once had, and could only once have had, a home. I didn't know; but the décor of this "lair" was depression writ large on every wall. I recalled the mess into which my old house descended during my dark nights of the soul …

"Bartle," I said, "I have tried to do what I can for you in a spirit of friendship and as your GP. I have tried to help you out of this horrible miasma in which your life seems to be mired. But I have reached my limit. I am beyond the end of my rope. I again ask, no, *beg*, that you allow me to refer you to a psychologist."

"I would prefer not to see a psychologist," he intoned like a scarred record rutted in its own desolation.

"Very well. This then must be the end of it."

And I left.

*

That night the great black bird returned. Now the jagged swooping shadow bore an eye, a green eye flecked with red, whose absent stare I tried desperately to fathom as the great mass descended, wings flinging me into the air …

I staggered into work and was just managing to get through my day when Pam said she was putting a call through to me. It was the police.

The sergeant explained that an hour earlier, a man had wandered out into the early morning traffic on Hoddle Street, apparently dazed or on drugs. Some cars had swerved to miss him but another, travelling at high speed, had killed him instantly. The man was as yet unidentified. The police were ringing me because the only possession found on the body was one of my appointment cards.

"Can you tell us who this man might be, doctor?"

"Yes," I said, "the man's name was Bartle Emmett. He was briefly a patient of mine but he would never tell me anything about his early life. He lived in a bedsit in Muir Street, Richmond. Number 15. He was, in my view, mentally ill, but was essentially a gentle person. I would appreciate it if you can pass on any information you may find and let me know the details of the funeral, if there is to be one." He assured me that he would.

As I put down the phone, a colossal fatigue engulfed me. I felt my chin drop to my chest. The room was stiflingly hot. Far off a great dark churning shape was coming towards me through baking, dusty air. I jerked myself awake. Clutching at the arms of the chair, I wondered how I would find my way home.

# Wasserman's Dream

Wasserman sank unsteadily into the orange chrome-framed chair. He took in the chocolate shagpile carpet, molasses-lacquer coffee table strewn with old magazines; posters and prints on beige walls. Commanding one wall was a large laminated medical diagram of the anatomical region that housed his deadly tumour. Networks of red, pink and blue lines, zones of orange, yellow, red and fleshy white, all labelled in minute black lettering. To the left hung a faded print of Van Gogh's *Sunflowers*, a photograph of a tree-shaded stream trickling through a rocky landscape, and a swirling orange, red, yellow and blue print of Munch's "The Scream", the screamer's cheekbones picked out in purple.

What the fuck is that doing in a doctor's surgery? he fumed to himself.

Wasserman was thin and slightly stooped. His lank white hair lapped the collar of his blue shirt. He had on a black leather jacket, jeans and running shoes.

His estranged wife had offered to accompany him to the appointment, but even for this, he could not let go of his rage at her.

They had no children. He went alone, as he felt, to the final frontier.

*

He had been in a rage all his life – at the Germans, at his clingy survivor mother with her veined, traumatized eyes; at himself. Gerald Wasserman was only fifty-five, but he was dying.

The surgeon had told him that he could learn more about the operation that, at best, would give him an extra nine to twelve months.

"The internet has entries, but stay with reliable sources – Harvard, the Mayo Clinic."

*Why the hell play it safe?* He was a dead man walking. He had nothing left to fear.

*

Back home, Doctor Google turned up not just explanations, but videos of the operation.

Three robotic arms appeared on the screen. Each wielded a pincer. A Stephen Hawking-like demonstration voice explained that two could incise, grab and apply suction. The third arm was for "manipulation and traction".

The right arm, assisted by the other two, started to slice, sweep and nudge away tissue like a Stanley knife vandalizing a spider's web. Behind every veil or globule of flesh appeared another, and another, and another, as the camera accompanied the pincers down an interminable cavern of flesh. Strange shapes loomed into view in the camera's spotlight: englobed enormities, things with serrated edges, pink and white stalactites suspended over underground rivulets of ooze, tubes glowing a dirty phosphorescent white, delicate latticeworks of blood vessels, large masses of tissue shoved aside or diced like mince. As these masses bulged into view they morphed into red fleshy octopus heads, indeterminate parts filamenting their way beyond the frame.

Wasserman was starting to feel faint, nauseous. A queasy headache was scrambling his thoughts. The hand that he knew should order the mouse to cancel the video was paralysed, dangling from a limb that did not seem to belong to him.

Roving beams as if from a deep-sea submersible were spotlighting open-jawed translucent monstrosities with rows of jagged needle-teeth, fanned tubular appendages protruding from head, back …

He watched in clammy horror, stunned by how far these pincered expeditionaries seemed to be travelling. How far could something so sharp travel in a human body? Was the body's inside warped like Einsteinian space? So much of the interior world could be shredded, torn asunder, done away with, and still leave a person breathing. Vast swathes of the inner world were inessential? Or would the rent veils dumbly self-repair, organs ooze back into place, gashes heal, violated nerves recompose?

Periodically the online surgeon, now sounding like a tormenter, would announce new stages in the process: "Dissection of seminal vessels."

"Dissection of anterior abdominal wall."

Now he was looking down at his own body, chained to the robotic apparatus as if to a machine of torture. All around lay great wastes of excremental filth, fleshy weeds climbing into the stinking smoky air, spectral figures bowed and broken by a great humiliation.

The vision gradually dissolved, its millions of pixels seeming to blur and fizzle out in darkness.

Wasserman circled dizzyingly down into his body.

The robotic voice and arms forged on.

Then the video ended, the surgeon's voice crackling in triumph as a lump of tissue – the prostate gland – tumbled into what could have been a kitchen colander.

Wasserman sat stunned in his desk chair, then lay down on a nearby sofa.

*

Wasserman, a financial planner, worked from home. He'd taken inordinate trouble over his office. Clean-lined, cool, minimalist. White walls. White lever-arched folders and small alphabetized clusters of books on off-white wooden shelving. Honey-coloured parquetry floor tiles reflected light from a feature window that looked out onto a silver gum, its grey-green leaves today vague shapes against a glowering sky. Lamps and vases sat on antique dressers on either side of the room. His large black and chrome L-shaped desk looked down the long rectangular space. At the exact mid-point of the walls to left and right hung two Mondrian prints, their grids of yellow, blue, red, black and white exuding geometric calm. Lamp shades, pen holders and other desktop appurtenances picked up Mondrian's primary colours. Smartly offsetting the black desk's opaque surface were his white laptop and a wandering Jew plant, its lilac and green leaves tendrilling their way down the side of a white vase.

At the far end of the room hung a very large print of Chagall's *Sur La Route du Village*. Wasserman loved the way its figures floated in green and blue fable-space, perspectives garbled as in a child's painting. The red rooster carrying two lovers gliding over the *shtetl* roofs. A vase of flowers hovering in the middle of the canvas, the woman with two children, her feet barely touching the mossy ground. He often found himself gazing at the Hassid at the bottom left of the painting, apparently journeying with his donkey through this magical, God-luminous landscape. He thought of Chagall's image as his "beyond", a serene place of the mind just out of his desperate reach.

*

"I can give you a few extra months but, I'm sorry – that's all I can do, and it's a big operation." The surgeon was a round-faced man with thinning blond hair and steel rimmed glasses.

Fury rising, Wasserman started to goad the man, to ply him with questions he thought him too vacuous to answer. "Should a man in terror of death seize every last moment, or should he just submit with grace?" asked Wasserman.

"That's a very personal question," replied the surgeon, blinking uneasily at Wasserman across the green leather expanse of his imitation antique desk.

The consulting room's white walls were lined with framed medical certificates. On the desk a gold tennis trophy, a framed family photo and a writing pad.

"How do your other patients take this sort of news?" asked the doomed man.

"Usually with much sadness, sometimes anger," replied the other, looking increasingly uncomfortable, "but my job is to tell people where they stand as regards their physical health and what I can do to help, if anything. I must leave the emotional side to others."

His head throbbing with rage, Wasserman ploughed on. "You see, doctor, as you gave me the news, a huge black canopy unfurled over us, cast a blinding shadow over your medical degrees, and then blotted out the world. Do you ever see black in your patients' eyes? Do you yourself ever see black?"

A long pause. "Well, as to my patients, I suppose I do see a sort of blackness in their eyes, but I have never really thought about it that way. As for me …"

Another pause. "I suppose I don't have time to look. I am an extremely busy man, Mr Wasserman."

"Perhaps you keep yourself busy so that you don't have to look," said Wasserman.

The surgeon stared back at him in disapproving amazement, his head turned slightly to one side. Then hesitantly he asked, "So what exactly *is* this blackness, Mr Wasserman?"

"It is death without a god," replied the patient in a matter-of-fact tone.

Another pause. "You say in your patient information that you are of the Jewish faith."

"I am Jewish," replied Wasserman, "but faith – after the Holocaust? I am a bad Jew."

"Still," said the doctor rising from his chair, making his way around the desk and gesturing towards the door, "there might be some guidance, some comfort, in talking to a rabbi? Perhaps rabbis see bad Jews even if bad Jews don't see rabbis?"

*

He was floating.

Below him were the roofs of Caulfield, St Kilda, Elsternwick. The terracotta tiled roof of his old friend Kranstein's house. At the front door the Hassidic face smiled warmly, but he looked far off, as if in a daguerreotype. Black suit trousers shiny with wear. Black kippa perched on wavy silver-grey hair. White *tzitzit* draped below his knees. Bushy beard flecked with grey.

They walked down a long white endless corridor, barren but for an image as vast as a billboard: the Lubavitcher Rebbe, Schneerson, stared down, fierce, implacable. The titan glowered Jewish indomitability from the ruins of the *shtetl* to suburban Melbourne, Australia.

"You are neither man nor Jew!" boomed the Patriarch. Wasserman shrank back.

It is true! It is true! he groaned.

He followed Kranstein through a flaming *chuppah* into his study. They sat facing each other. A pine bookshelf heaved under the weight of the Holy Books. Gold Hebrew letters danced on the black spines.

"What must we discuss?" asked Kranstein.

"Death," replied Wasserman. "I am in terror of death."

Kranstein replied in ecstatic tones, waving his arms and looking now up to the heavens and back to his friend. "We are creaturely. Born to pray, to live humble, obedient lives, and die. For a good Jew, death holds no terrors. We are creatures of God. To die the creaturely death – to die the death of one who knows himself a creature – is to know that you have played your part in something *so vast, so sublime, that you are in love with your own finitude!*"

The gold lettering blurred, danced, swept up to a pinnacle, then drifted down colourless and translucent like delicately veined cicada wings.

The Rebbe's face was in the room now. "You are neither man nor Jew!" "Neither man nor Jew!" he intoned, "Neither…"

*

Wasserman was standing before a colossal black iron fence. The liberal *shul*, Temple Beth Israel, soared up and up, its peak lost in eddying grey clouds. Its garden, a rocky field of cactus, moss and weed.

His bar mitzvah rabbi boomed, "Gerald Wasserman, you are now a man in the eyes of your faith. Think not of eternal life but of the eternal life of the *mitzvot*, the good deeds. The good Jewish life!"

Stained glass windows beamed swathes of colour onto serried congregants; their faces, now swept up in great tides of refracted colour, rushed towards him.

"Where is that man? Where is that man? Where is that man?" intoned the faces.

"My son *is* a man. A *good* man!" cried his mother, her veined eyes choked with horror.

An old photograph of his survivor father browned and curled in tongues of flame.

"Where is that man? I am not he!" cried Wasserman, clutching the fence, tears streaming down his face.

"He *cannot* be that man!" shouted Bloom, his psychiatrist, ringing his hands. "Freud and Hitler gave the Jews a new religion. When you're dead you're dead, and when you live, you live in dread."

A flame was dancing. Tall slit windows in a grey concrete wall. Steel struts wreathed in beseeching hands, machinery of annihilation, jagged steel fragments, barbed wire, Hebrew letters, edged up the walls like colossal insect legs. The Holocaust Museum.

The flame exploded. A vast wall of fire incinerated two thousand people, scores of his relatives, in the Great Synagogue of Bialystok, the mighty green dome buckling, melting, collapsing. Fire raging through arched windows.

Treblinka. Bodies stacked in heaps. Great stinking wastes.

Where is that man?

Neither man nor Jew!

*

Port Phillip Bay rippled, the breeze whitening wave tips as they rose and subsided.

He was sitting beside a white-haired balding man with thick wire-framed glasses and kindly blue eyes. It was his Uncle Moshe. Dead for twenty years. He'd got out of Bialystok and hidden in the forest. They were the same age now.

They sat, bodies touching on a bench looking out over St Kilda Beach. There was no sand. Mossy green stretched far into the distance, meeting waves lapping at the horizon. Gulls circled, some screeching for food, others frolicking in draughts of summer afternoon breeze.

"Vat is wrong, Gerald? You look so sad," Uncle Moshe asked.

"I am sick," said Wasserman, "I am dying."

"Ve must die like men," said his uncle.

"Like Jewish men?"

"There is nothing special about a Jew. Ve breathe uncertainty, ve live, ve die."

He turned to Gerald, put his hand on this shoulder, and went on, "For the old Jews you lived well. You helped ready the world for ze Redeemer. You died. Death vas nothing unless you died young and broke the parents' hearts. Died before you could do all ze *mitzvot.*"

"Hitler killed more than one-and-a-half million children," said Wasserman. "What chance did they have to be good Jews?"

The other nodded. "Ze Jews are like all ze persecuted peoples. They leave their bodies and see from high up vat this life is. The terror and the beauty. Maybe our human race is not fit for this planet. If a man says no to God, vy not? If he says no to life, vy not? But if he says yes, then he should not worry about his own death. Only about the death of the others who died seeing the horror, or did not live long enough to understand."

Wasserman gazed out across the green expanse. Far in the distance a group of men and women were wending their way along by the water's edge. On horseback rode two cloth-capped bearded men in boots, white shirts and woollen waist coats. *Tzitzit* bobbed at their sides. Women in headscarves and plain long brown skirts walked hand-in-hand with young children. A bearded man in black Hassidic garb walked with three untethered donkeys, waiting patiently as the animals stopped to graze. Dogs flew and yapped.

Wasserman turned to his uncle. But he was gone. A magnificent white gull with a mustard beak and jet-black eyes perched where Moshe had sat. A strange sombre luminosity lingered in the air. There was a gentle tapping at his shoulder. A young woman was selling bouquets of flowers. He reached towards her …

*

He came to on the sofa, crying, bathed in perspiration. The doomed feeling still clung to him, but the death-dread had lifted a little.

Not a dead man walking, perhaps, but a live man learning how to die …

The gum leaves at the window shone green against a lighter sky.

Mondrian's gentle geometry beckoned him through to the Chagall, now glowing in late afternoon light.

The Hassid with his donkey would go on his devout, creaturely way, death-dread transfigured by stories of what it means to die.

Wasserman picked up his phone and rang his wife.

# Balderstone's Salute

"He is an emissary of pity, and science, and progress, and
devil knows what else."
– Joseph Conrad, *Heart of Darkness*

Sooty clouds were rolling in from the South China Sea
across the evening sky. Hong Kong's nightly light show
had started its dance among the skyscrapers behind us;
multicoloured lights frilled the Kowloon coast ahead.

From our fish restaurant on the harbour in Causeway
Bay we watched the ferries shuttle between Kowloon
and the Island. Fishing boats old and modern, leisure
cruisers, junks and yachts had been returning to safe
harbour. Brightly lit tourist boats meandered  about
on the rippling tide. We wondered what was to come
of it all. The British had handed Hong Kong back to
the mainland Chinese five years earlier. Many Hong
Kongers had fled in fear of the totalitarian giant to the
north. Some observers declared it the very last gasp of
the British Empire.

The four of us – myself, William Lee, a lawyer; Henry
Fong, an eminent local businessman and patron of
the arts; James Koo, a pro-Democracy journalist; and
Bernard Chan, an economist and former university
president – were retired and had long been meeting

at this place to talk. Each brought a bottle of wine and time to imbibe plenty more.

Chan had been Professor of Economics at Oxford. He'd returned to Hong Kong as inaugural President of Mencius, a university far north in the New Territories. As a professional man he had been the very soul of discretion. Gossip stopped with him. His stories were comic, fanciful affairs delivered with whimsical good humour. He was a man of slight build with thinning hair and a narrow aquiline nose not common among us Chinese.

Latterly something had loosened in him. The old discretion had melted away. Not completely, but his stories had become more personal, and comedy, if it be there, was infused with anger or glum incredulity.

"The strangest Englishman I ever met," he began, "was a chap called Balderstone. He was from a coalmining town in Yorkshire; got a PhD in history at Durham University, then a teaching position of some sort there. He was a rather wild-looking fellow with a shock of unkempt red hair, a long ginger beard, and suspicious, hooded, cloudy blue eyes. He walked splay-footed and stooped. When he spoke his mouth drooped to one side. He had an extraordinary laugh which boomed like the roar of a wounded buffalo then trailed off in a high-pitched cackle. He dressed in a sort of one-man uniform – grey-blue shirt, grey-blue trousers, grey-blue cardigan, black walking shoes. The wide campus courtyard was attractively land-scaped – raised flowerbeds, fountains, ponds, miniature bridges – and rimmed by smart new blue-green buildings. Balderstone would stroll about there in his uniform, hatless even in blazing high summer.

"We had an urgent need for a nineteenth-century British historian and he seemed the perfect fit. He'd published a few articles in the area and had a book about Darwin and the clergy on the way with Oxford University Press. His reference from Durham described 'a man of considerable ability, enormous industry and the complexity that often drives high achievement.' Perhaps we didn't give that word – *complexity* – quite the attention it deserved; but Balderstone was also said to be a 'dedicated teacher with a particular commitment to assisting less-well performing students'; a commitment inherited from his mother who had been a remedial teacher in a Yorkshire school. Just what was needed for our working-class students! We hired Leonard Balderstone after a telephone interview in which he impressed with his determination to help our young university make its way in the world.

"This colourful man soon became a 'campus identity'; a creature of legend in our little community of three thousand. One of his British expatriate colleagues reckoned that Balderstone had been in heated dispute with Durham after it had declined to offer him a long-term position. I never got to the bottom of this story, perhaps because I didn't altogether want to.

"As was our custom, we held a little welcoming party for him. For the occasion he complemented his uniform with a black tie. He was friendly enough, as he had been in his first meeting with me a couple of days earlier. After a few drinks he became quite garrulous. When someone asked him about his parents, he replied, 'Both dead. My father was never going anywhere but the pub and a wooden box. My mother was a good woman but she should have left the drunken sod. So she got what she deserved, didn't she?'"

"Filial piety. Now there's a man who'd done his homework!" laughed Koo.

"Indeed," said Chan, "it struck the gathering dumb for a minute or two. Anyway, three months after his arrival Balderstone came to see me again. He had, he said, 'done an informal audit' of the History Department and had found it 'moribund'. Several of its twelve members 'lacked the ability to publish in reputable venues' and there was 'an absence of leadership, vision, of *will*, to pull the place up by its bootstraps.' He reminded me that his Darwin book was close to publication. It was all done with furtive glances left and right, as if checking for eavesdroppers. At times he spoke in lowered tones with a hand to the drooping side of his mouth as if funnelling his message to me alone."

Here Chan chuckled in his quiet way and gestured towards the wine bottle. "I was starting to get an inkling of his game. I am a tolerant fellow, as you know, but I was beginning to have doubts about this man. The Head of History, Jeremy Johnson, was a decent and efficient leader. True, he was not what you'd call dynamic, but he was working hard to build collegial spirit and initiative among what was indeed a rather mixed group. Soon I received an email from Balderstone 'summarizing' our previous discussion and reaffirming his desire to see the Department, 'take the great leap forward needed to see it challenge the history departments at Hong Kong University and the Chinese University of Hong Kong.'"

"A Maoist leap in Hong Kong!" quipped Fong. We all laughed.

"Next," Chan went on, "I received a dinner invitation from the man. I could have done without this, but it would have been bad form not to go. The Balderstones, a childless couple, lived in a large apartment at Gold Coast with sweeping views of the sea. From his study, lined, as he was at pains to show me, with history books, he could see the latter-day colonialist's panoply – junks, barges, huge ocean-going pleasure craft and ships wending their way under blue or often sooty skies. When typhoons were imminent, smaller craft would huddle in the marina below his window. Most of the furniture in the dining room was Chinese, though the couple had brought a few pieces from home. On a wall beside the table hung a vast artwork. It took me several minutes to work it out. Balderstone loathed this place's obsession with public signs."

"Who doesn't?" said Koo.

"Yes," replied Chan, "but it's *our* place. So," he continued, "he had photographed various specimens: beware big waves signs at calm beaches, stay-off signs beside well-grassed areas of parks, danger signs on walkways, on hiking trails etc., etc. He'd paid a photographer to arrange them into a montage. It must have been five square feet. His wife, Mary, a potter and a very nice woman (God help her!) said, 'President and Mrs Chan, I hope you realize that this is just Leonard's quirky British sense of humour. We both love Hong Kong.'

"'Where's your sense of humour, woman?!' snapped her husband. She made no further comment.

"The evening was more tolerable than I'd feared. Balderstone was a boisterous host. He could be very amusing (this, I think, is why colleagues who didn't much like him often sought his company). He said that Karl Marx teaches that 'history heals all wounds', and Groucho Marx that 'history wounds all heals'. He greeted his own joke with his booming buffalo laugh and cackle.

"Surprised by such levity from this source we laughed along with him.

"His most biting quips were reserved for his own country. The Queen was 'Her Mendacity', the leader of the Conservatives 'Michael Housefrau'. He said that if there was reincarnation the English cricket team would come back as lemmings. He loathed the British class system and the 'pink gin-swilling Westminster toffs who propped up her stinking carcass'.

"In a small university like Mencius most things wind up on the President's desk, including student satisfaction surveys. Most of the students wrote warmly of Balderstone's teaching, giving him high ratings on the clarity of his explanations, his availability, his entertaining lectures, and so on. Many looked up to him as a sort of father figure. And I believe that in his own way he did care about them. I'd see him in the canteen giving extra English tuition at lunch times. He apparently attended the formal dinners students held at big hotels and would give amusing speeches as Guest of Honour. But I made a concerned mental note of a few outlier responses: 'Mr Balderstone teach me much but <u>he should not shout!</u> It upset us!' 'Professor Balderstone try hard to make student better but sometime get so angry and red in face it stop us to concentrate.' 'Dr Balderstone sometime like my father who yell at me. Dr Balderstone try hard to teach me but I afraid when he lose temper.'

"Now Balderstone did something that seemed to trump such reports. He asked to see me with a student whose family 'was in crisis'. He arrived with a shy young man by the name of Leung. He explained that Leung's father, a heavy drinker, had deserted the family, leaving his mother to raise him and his autistic brother. Recently the mother had been diagnosed with breast cancer. They lived in a tiny apartment in Yuen Long and had been threatened with eviction. Balderstone, having researched the university's student aid schemes, urged – no *beseeched* – me to assist. I referred the case as a matter of urgency to our Student Aid Committee, with the desired result.

"Balderstone sent a brief note of thanks, which I appreciated. He also mentioned that he had been invited to speak in a few weeks at the Helena May Club. His topic was to be tertiary education in Hong Kong. I did not attend but got the gist of his remarks soon enough from a report in the *South China Morning Post*."

Chan extracted a laptop computer from its satchel. He had clearly been feeling impelled to share this tale with us and had come prepared.

"Under the headline 'A Lesson in Selflessness' Balderstone was quoted as saying that 'the European self, for all its faults, is nuanced and layered; the Chinese self is thin by comparison and has little capacity for introspection'. He added that 'it is up to our universities to resist further erosion of the Hong Kong self at the hands of our totalitarian overlords to the north. But it is doubtful whether the stuff-shirted sycophants who people the local Education Board will have the wit or spine to act.'"

"Talk about the European in an eastern colony!' said Fong, laughing. "A perfect specimen!"

We clinked glasses and ordered our meals.

"This, of course, was well before the radicalization of Hong Kong students, but ours often told me that they treasured their 'East-West identities'. Most would not have taken exception to Balderstone's remarks.

"I called Balderstone in and said, 'Leonard,' – yes, I found myself addressing him with increasing familiarity – 'you can express your views on important cultural issues, but *we cannot have abusive public references by Mencius staff to the Education Board!* The Board determines our funding and many other aspects of our existence, as you well know. Do you *hear* me? What possessed you, a man so committed to this university's future, to *say* such things?!'

"He looked at me with all the concern of a man flicking a breadcrumb from his jacket and said, 'I really can't say, Bernard. The mysteries of human motivation …'

"I felt so provoked that I told him the next warning he received would be an official one.

"He replied, 'Mr President, I hear you, and who could not be better for that experience?'

"This insolence was delivered with a completely straight face. I was speechless. I gestured to the door and watched him make his nonchalant way out.

"Next day came an email from a staff member in the Counselling Service." Chan located the document on his iPhone.

> Dear President Chan, after careful consideration I must write to you about Ms Alice Pang, a first-year student at Mencius University.
>
> Ms Pang has been seeing me for six months about her unhappy home life. She also lacks confidence at university. Like most of our students she is the first from her family to attend university.
>
> Ms Pang works very hard and receives encouragement from her mother. But her father is the traditional Chinese father. When Ms Pang was born he would not visit his wife in the hospital because the baby was a girl. He does

not take any interest in Alice and has a violent temper. One time he threw her laptop computer out of the window. A few weeks ago Alice and the mother had to sleep in the car because he came home drunk and hit Mrs Pang.

Ms Pang does not have good training for university but she works hard and asks advice from her teachers.

Last week she knocked on the door of her History teacher, Dr Leonard Balderstone. He had given her 40% on an essay. She wanted to know how she could do better next time. Ms Pang says that at first Dr Balderstone was quite friendly. He tried to show her what was wrong with some of her sentences; but when she could not fix them, he went red in the face, shouted that she "has the mind of a twelve-year-old", screwed the essay up and threw it in the bin. Ms Pang ran out of the room. Yesterday she came to me in tears.

Since then she has stayed mostly in her dormitory room.

"Can this be the same man who came to you with young Leung?" I asked in amazement.

"Yes, the very same, Lee. How that can be I do not know. The man shook my confidence in the knowledge of the human heart." He smiled ruefully and refilled his glass. "I referred the matter to David Yang, the Dean of Students, and told him not to put up with any nonsense. He was to tell Balderstone that further such incidents would trigger an official sanction.

"Next day, Yang rather sheepishly reported that the interview had been 'water off a duck's back'. Balderstone had told him that our students 'were raised to bow, scrape, obey and never ask questions. You cannot do history if you can't think for yourself'. Then he added, 'Sometimes you need to rattle their cages for their own good.'"

An audible gasp went round the table.

"Balderstone apparently carried a sort of filter around with him. He just filtered out anything that wasn't grist to the mill of his exorbitant ambition. This power of forgetting let him keep his eye on the prize. But a man who cannot remember cannot learn. He was a colonial Sisyphus pushing the same colossal rock uphill wherever he went.

"He now proposed a grand plan – a university-wide English literacy subject that would occupy a third of the students' tuition time. He brought his proposal to our biggest committee, the Academic Board. Presentations to the Board were usually limited to twenty minutes, but he spoke for forty-five.

"Among other things he claimed that, 'Student English at this university is so appalling that staff can be little more than glorified school teachers and students can barely follow simple explanations in their language of instruction.'

"Colleagues were stunned. Michael Tang, Head of English, rose and said, 'Dr Balderstone, thank you for the work you have put into your proposal, but it is surely excessive. English is our students' second language. All Hong Kong universities have these problems. As for glorified high school teachers – if you consult Mencius publication data you will find that many of your colleagues have international scholarly reputations.'

"Thunderous applause. Balderstone, his face scarlet, his mouth horribly twisted, shouted, '*Of course* Dr Tang and his colleagues in the English Department take no responsibility for this mess. They'd rather teach their beloved high literature while their students read plot summaries on the internet! Our students need to be studying fifteen hours per day, as they do on the mainland.' With this he stormed out.

"This resulted in an extended entry in what Human Resources came to call The File – Balderstone's rapidly expanding staff dossier. He was called to a meeting with myself and others and given his first formal warning for creating a 'hostile and intimidatory work place environment'. Three warnings and the university has grounds for dismissal."

"How did he take it?" I asked.

"With complete insouciance. He simply said, 'I must try to get up every morning a better man, mustn't I?'

"When the formal proceedings were over he asked for a private word with me. Before I had a chance to refuse, he pulled a book out of a brown paper bag and proudly handed it to me. It was *Darwin and the Provincial Clergy: a collection of letters and documents*, by Dr Leonard Balderstone, Associate Professor of

History, Mencius University, Hong Kong. Oxford University Press no less! He gestured to me to look inside the cover of the handsome tome. There he had written:

To Bernard, leader, mentor and friend,
In grateful appreciation, Leonard

"I ask you – what is a man to do in such a situation?" We shook our heads.

"The History Department performed very badly in that year's research grants and promotions rounds. Not one History staff member was promoted and only Balderstone received a grant. Poor Johnson was dismayed and decided to take study leave. I wanted to appoint Joseph Yam, a popular colleague, as Interim Head, but Balderstone started lobbying for the position. I know all about this because, like a fool, he did some of his lobbying in emails which, unbeknownst to him, were forwarded to me."

Again, he read from his laptop.

"He offered himself as the 'dynamic leader who could forcefully represent the Department in the higher councils of the University', could 'restore respect for the Department that was currently seen as a laughing-stock on campus', and could 'put the necessary weight behind promotion applications to ensure a high rate of success.'

"He and several colleagues then took Yam out for dinner and got the poor man so inebriated that he agreed to step aside for Balderstone. By the time Yam had hauled himself out of bed late the next morning an email from – guess who? – and countersigned by ten History staff had landed in my inbox."

He read the document out to us from his iPhone.

> Dear President Chan,
>
> Staff of the Mencius History Department have been extremely disappointed by the Department's lack of recognition in the recent funding and promotion rounds. They have prevailed upon me as its most successful researcher and one with perceived leadership ability to put myself forward as Interim Head of the Department, should you see merit in this suggestion. Dr Yam, who of course has the best interests of the Department at heart, has acceded to this proposal.
>
> Yours faithfully,
>
> Dr Leonard Balderstone etc.

"When I phoned him, Yam confirmed that he had agreed to the proposal. 'Who would want to be Head of a department that had Leonard Balderstone in it?' he remarked."

"Indeed," said Fong, "you might as well agree to herd cats."

Chan continued, "Now began a program of activity that would have done a UN reconstruction project justice. Balderstone introduced regular staff seminars for discussions of staff research, visiting lectures by eminent academics; he launched a fortnightly departmental newsletter, each issue with a Head's Note, that listed all staff activity for the preceding weeks. Each issue of the newsletter was forwarded to me so that I could see the great strides the Department was making. There were to be departmental drinks, meals; even hiking trips!"

"Some of this sounds quite reasonable," said Fong.

"Indeed," replied Chan, "but the annual staff appraisals now became due. The process required the Head and the staff member to sign off on the Head's appraisal of the staff member's performance. But Balderstone, unbeknownst to his staff, wrote supplementary comments which were much harsher than the ones that had been agreed upon. He forwarded these with the appraisals to Human Resources. Though untrustworthy himself, Balderstone always seemed to believe that others – even those he might have given reason to dislike him – would keep his confidences. Perhaps it was one of the curators of The File who spilled the beans.

"In his ascent to the Headship Balderstone had made common purpose with Dr Zhao Ma, a bright but explosive mainlander. Ma had lost family and colleagues in the Cultural Revolution. He had been forced to abandon a promising academic career at Peking University and tend poultry in a remote northern province. Until recently Ma and Balderstone had been at daggers drawn; but Balderstone vouched unconditional support for Ma's career advancement.

"A group of History students were studying in a vacant classroom in the Department when they heard shouting from the room next door. 'You're a devil!

A *gweilo*! You had *no right* to do that! It is not in the regulations!' yelled one man.

"'I was elected to...' began the other.

"'You were *not* elected! You wriggled your way in like a snake. You said you would help us. But you betrayed us!'

"'I was *appointed* to improve the performance of this department – a service to all its members!'

"'How was that a service?! Who are you to judge us? You are just an old-fashioned index card historian!'

"'*Am I now?!* Well, when you publish with Oxford you can pass judgement on *me*. Meanwhile I suggest you get back to your chickens!'

"The students reported the ruckus to the Dean who reported it to me. I replaced Balderstone as Interim Head with Yam. Staff were assured that Balderstone's supplementary assessments had been ignored. Balderstone was given a second formal warning. Again, he appeared unconcerned about the warning itself, but Ma's jibe about the sort of historian he was had clearly hit a bare nerve.

"'No-one calls me *that!*' he fumed. 'Where he comes from, they don't even *have* history. All they have is Party propaganda.'

"Again, he asked to stay behind for a chat. Proudly announcing that his book had received an excellent review in the *Times Literary Supplement*, he handed me a xerox of it, replete with another handwritten dedication. By now I knew his game. I just gestured towards the door.

"Balderstone now became a rather pitiable figure. He was a pariah among his own staff, and widely disliked by others; his wife had apparently gone home to look after her elderly mother. His beard hung down his chest and his hair had coiled into ropy knots. People never knew which Balderstone they were going to get – a wildly excited one who talked and talked, or a morose, monosyllabic one who eyed others with suspicion. When in a good mood, he would pull out a recorder he carried with him and play *Auld Lang Syne* in the courtyard. In a lecture he once likened himself to Napoleon at Saint Helena.

"One day an American exchange student by the name of Leibowitz was videoing scenes of Mencius campus life. After surveying the courtyard with his camera, he settled on a group of five students sitting at a long table festooned with banners and balloons. They were recruiting freshmen to join the university debating society. Footage of one of the previous years' debates ran on a loop on a projector screen; a large plastic hammer and a set of scales sat upon a wooden lectern. The kids at the table were performing a traditional campus ritual with earnest efficiency. A stooped Caucasian man with a splayed-footed gait now shuffled into the video frame. The man clicked his heels together and made a Nazi salute. The students, not knowing what to make of the gesture, giggled at this latest piece of theatricality from a familiar campus figure.

"Liebowitz, a Jew, knew that Hong Kong has seen little anti-Semitism. The Chinese of course have always admired the Jews' financial acumen. The young man reported the incident to the rabbi of the congregation he had been attending, Rabbi Levi. The rabbi rang me to report the incident and to ask whether the staff member might be teaching Holocaust denial. We made careful inquiries and found no evidence of it."

"Do you think he had fascist sympathies?" I asked.

"I don't *think* so," Chan said. "But perhaps there is a fine line between sympathies and tendencies in a case like this?"

We all pondered this.

Chan continued, "Once again, I summoned Balderstone to my office, saying merely that there was a 'matter of conduct' I wanted to discuss. Meanwhile I obtained a copy of the video from young Liebowitz, had a screen positioned beside my desk in my office, and ran the video for members of Council and the senior administration. It was decided that it constituted grounds for dismissal.

"Next day, Balderstone strode nonchalantly into my office and had begun booming pleasantries when he saw that my back was turned and that I was watching something on a screen. I could hear him stop stock-still. He said nothing. When the video had finished I got up and faced him.

"'Are you a fascist sympathizer, Balderstone?' I asked.

"'No', he replied in a chastened voice, 'I am not.'

"'Then why *on earth?!'*

"He stood, head bowed, one side of his mouth drooping like a man with the palsy. All the life had gone out of him. Something had at last got through to him. He shrugged his shoulders and said, 'I really don't know.'

"I was surprised to find at that moment that one can feel loathing and pity towards someone in the same instant. But I stood up, glared at him and said, 'Balderstone, let me tell you something about myself ... A certain Jewish woman escaped Vienna in 1943. She travelled overland to the Jewish ghetto in Shanghai. She married a Chinese trader. They had a son who married a Chinese woman. That couple had a son. That son is me.'"

"There was a long silence. He looked down at the floor, eventually raised his head, and said 'I see', turned and let himself quietly out. His resignation letter arrived an hour later. I never saw him again."

"Do you know what became of him?" Koo asked.

"He returned to England and taught in a public school. After a flaming row with the Headmaster, he stormed out of the Head's office, collapsed in the school courtyard and died of a massive stroke."

There was silence around the table. Then Fong asked, "And how was that *TLS* review?"

Chan pulled it out of his brief case and replied, "He had underlined one sentence for me: 'This book represents a prodigy of research whose collection and arrangement of documents will be an invaluable aid to scholars for years to come.' But the rest made clear that Balderstone had just done the digging. Others would have to make something of what he'd found."

"An old-fashioned index card historian, perhaps?" Koo suggested.

"It would seem so," replied Chan.

It was late and the gaiety had gone off the evening. The moon cast a filmy glow on the lapping water.

We made our way out. Chan and I took a taxi east to our apartments. The Causeway Bay streets were thronged with late-night life. As the taxi sped along Long Wo Road we caught fleeting glimpses between apartment and office blocks of the moon-dappled harbour. Then on our right, its pedestal base bathed in a blinding yellow glow, the Chinese Liberation Army Building thrust into view, a towering gold rectangular column pulsing fiery shards into the midnight air.

# Starting Over

I'd come down to Florida after the operation to start over. The cancer wasn't in my bones, but the other thing was. The other thing that had chaperoned me out of my marriage and into early retirement from a community college out on Long Island. The medical prognosis was excellent, but that didn't seem to make any difference.

I'd put my Village apartment up for rental and taken a long-term lease on a condo in a gated community on a golf course by the sea in northern Florida. The beach was nice but mansions soared up off the dunes – Gone with the Wind monstrosities, great pink Spanish Revival birthday cakes, rambling Nantucket stone piles, angular postmodern extrusions of stone and steel. Later that year a monster hurricane ripped down that coast, flooding houses at sea level and leaving others hanging off sheer sand cliffs.

It was coming into summer and there were already lots of people on the beach. Some shuffled strangely about in the wet sand, heads down, foraging with their toes for something they'd stoop to pick up and examine. It turned out they were looking for sharks' teeth, which washed up in huge numbers there and which they used for bracelets, necklaces and other fineries. They weren't big, but curved, razor sharp, and the length of a thumbnail, they could tear flesh from bone. These people could be collecting sharks' teeth one minute and lolling about in the waves the next. Wouldn't a carpet of teeth suggest a sizable population of sharks? Not to these people, apparently. I determined to do my swimming in the estate pool.

I was accompanied on my long walks by a little rescue dog I'd gotten when I moved down there. He'd stay close unless he saw another dog. Then he was off butt-sniffing and wheeling in clouds of sand.

One day I saw a knot of people just by the water's edge. They weren't foraging. They were watching a fisherman, leant back as if against a gale, his rod bowed almost to breaking. Their eyes would flit from him to the place perhaps fifty yards out where the line disappeared into the water. A sinewy, bronzed man of middle age, bare-chested and streaming with sweat, he seemed mesmerized by the thrill of the chase, though, standing close to him, the little yapping dog now cradled in my arms, I thought I saw a hint of concern in his adrenalized brown eyes.

Suddenly the line went absolutely wild as a grey-white finned shape lifted above the waves, thrashed frantically, then dove down again. The crowd gasped.

"Jesus!" shouted the fisherman, "what a monster!"

The line quieted some, convulsed again, eased off, for longer this time, then pinged again into frenzied tension.

Eventually the fisherman, standing straighter, started warily to reel the thing in. About thirty yards out, a fin broke the surface and then the sleek grey-white back of a sizable shark's body. My mind, expecting the usual bullet-like head and pointy snout, went into a kind of free-fall as a T-shaped face rose up out of the water, its eyes goggling on rigid stems inches from the sides of its head. Tucked well back as if lying in wait under the T was the curved, pincered mouth of a shark. Later I remembered having seen photographs of creatures like this.

"Holy shit!" shouted the fisherman, "I'm not messing with that brute!" and, handing the rod to a startled young man, he dashed over to a wicker basket, pulled out a large fishing knife, dashed back and, holding the line steady in one hand, carved the creature free. It darted off. The crowd ooh'd and watched it for as long as its now dark shape could be seen streaking beyond the shallows, then started to disburse, some relieved, others wishing they'd seen the creature close up in its death throes on the sand.

I set the little dog down and stood for a while steadying my mind. When I looked up he was yards off, hurtling through the sand with another dog. I strode after him and came up to a woman who was delightedly filming the romp on her iPhone.

"Aren't they cute?!" she cried to me. "That one yours?"

"Yes it is."

"They're the same. Both terriers! And it's like they know it!"

"Well maybe," I replied, "but they're certainly cute."

Indeed they were fun to watch, though fun had become a sort of abstraction, something I knew existed but couldn't quite feel.

"I haven't seen you before. You live down here?" she asked.

"Yes, I just moved down here from New York. Did you see that shark the guy almost pulled in back there? You wouldn't want to run into that in the water."

"Yeah," she said, "just south of here one of those took a girl's arm off."

"So why do people swim here? The beach is littered with sharks' teeth!"

She stared at me as if I'd just asked the most idiotic question imaginable. Then she was off again chattering about the dogs.

"Look at them over there with that Great Dane! They make it look like a horse!"

As she looked at them I looked at her. She was tallish, bronzed, probably in her mid-forties, with broad, slightly bony shoulders and a lithe, beautiful figure. She was wearing something turquoise that could have been a bathing suit or maybe tennis gear, with a frilled skirt that stopped part way down her willowy thighs. Her blondish hair was tied back with a burgundy felt ribbon behind a sky-blue baseball cap. There was an odd gaiety about her blue eyes as if they were calibrated only to see fun.

Since the operation, I hadn't been looking at women in the old way, but now, despite my irritation at what I took to be her fake friendliness, something in me stirred.

She asked, "So how long are you down here for?"

"As I said, I'm down here permanently. I moved down from New York after cancer surgery to cheer myself up and make a new start."

"Oh, I had cancer surgery too. A melanoma right between my shoulder blades. Played havoc with my tennis for months. I'm Jill. My doggy is Jinx."

"I'm Elijah, and my pooch is Josh."

"Jinx and Josh, ha? Those two are going to have the best time! We should give them lots of walks together. What's your cell?"

We exchanged numbers and parted. Now familiar with the bubbly local friendliness that felt wholly insincere, I doubted she'd be in touch. And why would a local beauty like her want to spend time with a recently-arrived curmudgeon at least twenty years her senior?

*

Mornings were worst. The thing in my bones – the depression – had oozed its bilious vacuity into every corner of me overnight. I'd wake from nightmares feeling like a condemned man in a cell. In the dream, I'd turn up to give lectures on things I knew nothing about in languages I couldn't speak, I'd be lost in alien landscapes, my iPhone locked against my frantic tapping. The little dog, who felt like a part of me, would be missing among the dunes, or loose on a highway.

And then there were the Judy dreams, my estranged wife, now liberated from the toils of my melancholy, parading through these hellscapes with a paragon of manhood on her arm.

I'd lie there weighing the merits of the sickly coziness of bed and its risk of slipping back into nightmare against the buffeting discomforts of getting up. A strong coffee and then I'd start thinking about the shape of the day. Problem was, these days didn't really have a shape and I felt unable to impose one.

Sometimes I'd walk the pooch down to the local Starbucks. One patron, a Trump supporter indignant about "liberal media fake news", claimed to have been a realtor. Virtually every woman I met in the area claimed to be a realtor, and most of them were fake blondes; but she was a former fake blonde whose hair had finally conceded to white. She loved my dog, who'd sit on my lap as I sipped my coffee, so I cut her some slack.

I'd wander back, have lunch, then email friends and, God forbid, Judy, who couldn't let go of me – *me*, the very person she held responsible for all her unhappiness! But I felt the same way about her and I couldn't let go either. What was the deal? Those daily exchanges drove me deeper and deeper into gloom.

This particular morning I was still in bed when a text message announced itself with a ping: "Hey! Wanna walk the dogs later? Say 3?"

Well, I got that wrong, I thought, but could I be bothered?

It was almost 10 a.m. If I did Starbucks, lunch and skipped Judy, the accompanied walk would at least make for a change. So I tapped "Sure" and was waiting for her on the beach when she arrived.

*

"Sorry I'm late," she said.

"But you're not late," I replied, pointing to my iPhone that said precisely 3 p.m.

"Yes I am. I'm always late." The dogs had scooted off and we started after them.

"So," I ventured, "what's your line of crime?"

"*Ha?!*" she said, apparently taking this literally.

"Sorry, what I mean is, what do you do for a career? Most women have careers nowadays."

"I'm a realtor."

"Oh *really?* This place seems to be teeming with lady realtors."

"It's teeming with real estate," she said, "and with people who can afford to pay for it."

"So what sorts of property do you deal in?"

"Well, see that house over there," and she gestured towards a pink nouveau Spanish colossus that meandered on and on over a cattle ranch of a block and upwards for three storeys, "I'm talking with the guy who lives there. He's a lawyer and his two kids have moved out and it's too big for just him and his wife. They want to downsize."

Several snide rejoinders came to mind, but I didn't have the heart.

We wandered on to where the dogs were sprinting along the water's edge. She looked delightedly at them and reached for her iPhone. I looked at her. She was wearing a skirted outfit like the previous day's, this time in pale blue with a black baseball cap. She was statuesque even when standing at an odd angle to video the dogs and appeared to float across the sand that I trudged through. We seemed to be living in parallel universes.

Though I reckoned there probably wasn't much to know about this woman, I found myself wanting to know more. I'd noticed a large diamond ring on her wedding finger the day before, so now I inquired, "I guess you're a family woman as well as a realtor?"

"Yep, three kids – me and a husband. That makes five. You?"

"I'm separated. No kids."

After a long pause had elicited no further information I asked about her kids, each of whom turned out to be of college age. One, the oldest boy, was studying commerce, the girl was training to be a physiotherapist, and the youngest boy was "bumming around". She spoke at some length about where they were at in their lives, how often they came home for visits, and so on. And then another long pause.

For some reason I wasn't all that keen to know too much about her still anonymous husband, but I did ask her what he did.

"He's a lawyer. That's how come I'm talking to the guy in the big house. He's a colleague."

We walked on. In New York I didn't know anyone who would even think of voting for Trump, but down there just about everyone I met was intending to, and I'd got into a habit of asking why with only thinly concealed condescension. I angled the question with some care this time: "So how do you like the thought of having your first female President?"

"I could care less about the sex of the president," she replied. "I just want a good president. Not someone like Clinton. She carries on about how much she does for children and then she's pro-choice. Give me a break! Plus she's got a criminal record the length of your arm."

I was too flat to contest any of this and settled for, "Well, that sounds like a point in favor of Trump."

That evening I received a text. No words. Just an image. It had been crafted with loving care in a grainy sepia finish. From each of its edges a brownish orange shade began modulating into lighter and lighter shades of orange until the orange spilled over into a large bright oval-shaped pool of yellowy-orange light. At the back and to the left of the oval sat a grizzled brown-orange alpha lion. Superimposed on the creature was a yellow-orange profile of Trump, looking more leonine than the lion and sublimely unconcerned about anything that might get in his way. Beneath the profile, which oddly ended at his jaw line, and under the paws of the lion, oozed an elongated oval of red. Trump's eyebrow-crested gaze directed the viewer to the right of the image and to the words A LION DOESN'T LOSE

SLEEP OVER THE OPINION OF SHEEP. And below that, in a box, MAKE AMERICA GREAT AGAIN.

I reckoned that whoever had fashioned this had a fair grounding in fascist iconography. Not that Jill would have a clue about that. But what was her point? Was she trying to get under the skin of a "northern liberal", or could she have somehow thought I was pro-Trump? Either way, I really wasn't interested in pursuing the acquaintanceship.

*

I now embarked on a period of solitary withdrawal, rather as spurned prophets retreat to the desert, except that this was suburban Florida. I'd avoid Starbucks and the beach, taking our walks on the concrete path that girdled the golf course. Josh and I would wind up in the air-conditioned pro shop where I'd admire new clubs and crisp course attire, and where the club pro who served behind the counter would reply to my "How's it going?" with "Another day in Paradise."

Another denizen of that parallel universe.

I'd sit in my condo, savoring what Rebecca West calls "the savage peace ... to be found in the contemplation of doom." I'd play solitaire for hours on end, take malicious pleasure in not returning Judy's emails and follow-up phone calls, send jaunty, sardonic messages to friends and to my sweet sister, Milly, in Vermont. And I'd watch hours of CNN to be promised that Trump could not possibly win because only his "base" – those disaffected white working-class males –

would vote for him. But I was living in one of the best-heeled postcodes in the country and most of the men and women I was meeting there were planning to vote for him.

I was pleased not to have heard from Jill, though I'd find myself checking my phone for texts from her. What was she playing at? Was that Trump image some kind of test or, as I now suspected, a farewell slap?

After a week of silence I found myself texting her: "Long time no walk. Were you taken by a shark?"

Her reply was almost instantaneous: "Hurt my Achilles at tennis. Can't walk on sand. Coffee at Zac's? Dog friendly. Water bowls." I felt my spirits lift a little.

Zac's was a smart coffee and cake shop in an upmarket shopping strip across the highway, nestled among boutiques, furniture stores, hairdressers, wine bars, restaurants and galleries. As you approached, piped music – generally crooners and movie themes – becalmed you from speakers artfully secreted among plastic shrubs and palms. I got there a bit before four, our arranged meeting time. She was there at four pronto.

"Sorry I'm late."

"You're not late."

"Yes, I am. I'm always late. It's my one weakness."

"Whatever you say."

We tethered the tail-swishing dogs within sniffing distance of one another to the legs of white wrought iron chairs and sat down with our coffees, looking out into a manicured small garden at the back of the café.

Nothing was said, until I asked her about her injury. She said it was nothing, but she hated missing tennis, and made it clear that she wanted to move on to other topics. Another pause.

Feeling mildly rebuffed and cross, I thought I'd try something to breach her detachment. "So, what's your husband's name?"

"Lennie."

Pause.

"Nice guy?"

"I guess."

Pause.

This time I offered nothing to break the silence. She looked out into the garden. As the dogs supplicated for scraps, I looked at her.

Then she said, "So what's with you and your wife? Will she move down here?"

"No. I moved down here so that we'd be well away from each other. It would be nuts for her to move down here. And anyway, she loathes Florida."

"What's to loathe about Florida?! Maybe you'll move back up there?"

"You must have missed what I just said?"

"Maybe."

I wanted to shift the focus back to her. "So do you enjoy your real estate work?"

"It's good because you meet a lot of people and you do deals. Deals are like a chase. It's a buzz when you get one done. And you see inside lots of beautiful houses. But realty in an area like this has a real downside."

"How so?"

"Well, look around you, Elijah. Most people who come here come to die."

"Surely not," I said. "They've come to retire. They'd be counting on a long new lease on life and they can afford to pay modern medicine to give them one."

"Modern medicine!" she said, sneeringly.

Pause.

"Anyway, if lots of people die you get lots of properties to sell. Right?"

Pause.

Then, "One day I went to see an old lady who wanted to sell her condo and move into a retirement village. The appointment was for 11 and I was a few minutes late. Her maid took me through this glamor living room with gilt mirrors, chandeliers French furniture, down a passage and let me into the woman's TV lounge. The old lady was sitting in an armchair and when she looked up at me I almost passed out. Her face was gone!"

"What?!"

"I mean she had eyes and a mouth but her nose was gone and she had like plastic plates for cheek bones. She looked at me – two eyes sitting in flat plastic discs and two holes for nostrils."

"So how did she react?"

"She didn't bat an eyelid. She just said, 'I'm sorry, dear, I didn't know you were here already. I'll just put my face on,' and she picked up a sort of mask with a nose, skin and cheekbones, fastened it around the back of her head with a strap and said, 'There we are. That's better. Now I can start my day.' I was almost holding on to furniture so as not to faint, but she couldn't care a damn about that. All she cared about was getting her day started."

"Well, I guess she'd been through a lot – maybe a facial tumor, or burns – and she had taught herself to act casual about her disfigurement."

"That's not the point. She should have been more careful. Made sure she had her face on by the time I arrived. We live in a society with other people. Christian charity begins with feeling for others."

I'd never known her so heated, and the gloss had gone right off her gay manner. Her tanned knuckles were white around her coffee cup and she was looking determinedly away. I thought maybe she was misting-up, but I couldn't tell.

After a particularly long pause we started chatting about the dogs and she cheered up. "Give my regards to your wife," she said, presumably jokingly, as we parted and agreed to meet next time at the beach.

*

Nothing from her for a few days and then: "Hey! Meet at the beach at 5? Lennie can get home from work early and join us."

I was expecting a relaxed, upbeat sort of guy but the man with Jill – black wavy hair greying at the temples, an aquiline nose, narrow brown eyes – had the mien of a storm cloud. His smile as he shook hands was more like a sneer. As he made eye contact, he held his head back and slightly to one side and squinted. He appeared completely remote from Jill. He strode out ahead of us. She walked rapidly after him and when she caught up, they seemed to exchange heated words. He then hovered within range while I rejoined them. I tried to engage him but got mainly grunts and monosyllabic replies. His longest response came when in desperation I chanced a reference to the election campaign.

"Barbarians at both sides of the gate," he snorted.

Presently he broke away again and made towards the dogs who were sniffing and leg-cocking around a rotting tree trunk that had washed up at the back of the beach.

I wondered what this cheerful blonde was doing with a man like him. Maybe she'd been too conventional to make smart romantic choices? Maybe she did actually have a thing for curmudgeons? I felt sorry for Jill who'd quite lost her customary vivacity as she tried intermittently to mollify the man and establish a modicum of civility. She was almost dragging herself through the sand, stooped over, ignoring the dogs and casting occasional apologetic glances at me.

At one point when the husband wasn't looking, I gave her an encouraging nod. I had no idea whether this was appropriate or not. She responded with a resigned, wan smile. I sensed she was both sorry and pleased to have me there; that in some obscure way I had become important to her. But why? I'd been told that my inner desolation could look like calm. Maybe that was it. Maybe she saw in me – *me!* – some measure of soothing composure? Maybe ... These walks were clearly not just to exercise the dogs.

The husband seemed to cheer up briefly when romping with the dogs. He'd chase them along the water's edge, dart away from them provoking them to chase him, and throw a tennis ball as far as he could launch it. He never looked back to share the moment with Jill. Perhaps only the dogs could touch this side of him.

Then without saying a word, he turned and started back from whence we'd come. Jill glanced at me to see whether I wanted to walk back with them. I said I'd keep going for a ways. Needed the exercise. And when a minute later I glanced back over my shoulder, she was striding fast, trying to catch up with him.

*

Jill said nothing about that incident. Indeed she now seemed to be putting our acquaintanceship into a sort of reverse, keeping me at a greater distance with a constant stream of chatter about the dogs, the weather, real estate. I knew she was hurting and so didn't take any of this personally.

Well, actually, I did. I felt shut out, hurt, as if I wasn't trusted to converse without crossing some sort of line. I knew I should let her keep herself comfortable, even if there was some small cost to me. But I didn't. I needed a bit more from her.

Trump had by now won the election. She'd said nothing about it. Not even a text. But being angry at her for supporting him and angry in general, I asked, "So you got your guy into the White House. How do you think he'll go?"

She didn't miss a beat. Just looked straight ahead and said in a completely neutral tone. "I guess we'll see."

That was it. The silence that followed roused me to cross the line. "So how are things in general in your world?'

"Steady as she goes." And then, "How are things with your wife?"

"Just as they were. They won't change."

"Funny. You'd don't seem like a bad guy."

"As the novel says, 'you don't have to be a bad guy to depress somebody.'"

"What novel?"

"*Catcher in the Rye* by Salinger."

"Oh yeah, I read that at college. So, how often do you speak with your wife?"

"If you count emails, most days."

"So, it's not a real separation is it? It's a fake separation."

She turned to me and smiled ever so demurely. "Not bad for a dumb blonde, ha?" she said.

"No," I replied, "not bad at all. Quite good, in fact."

She smiled the same smile, and then we walked on for a quarter hour in silence until we were back to where we generally parted ways. I was about to say the usual "Thanks for the walk" when she took a step towards me, raised herself on tiptoes and gave me a little peck on the cheek, then strode off towards the car park without looking back.

After she'd gone from sight I turned and looked out over the shoreline. Beyond the fossickers a flat green-blue sea, slightly ruffled by the breeze, stretched out to the horizon under a cloud-wisped deep-blue sky. It was so quiet that the voices of those lounging about or tossing balls in the water were clearly audible. Josh was snuffling about with another dog and there was no reason to go back to the condo any time soon.

*

Nothing from Jill for a week. Surprise, surprise! I was cross – albeit, perhaps, in a faintly fond sort of way – and now reckoned myself on firm enough ground to break the silence. But then a text arrived: "Today at 3?"

This time, for the first time, she really was late. Twenty-five minutes late. I wanted to start walking but didn't want to disappear from sight and have her miss me and go home; so to Josh's surprise I'd walk several hundred yards up shore and then back again. Eventually I saw her striding fast towards me through the sand. For the first time ever she looked out of place there. No Jinx. The beach and tennis gear had gone. She had on a black skirt, a crisp white collared shirt and carried black stilettos in her hands. Her hair was gathered back in a tight bun. She looked distracted. More than distracted, almost beside herself.

"Sorry," she said, and started to walk fast along our customary route.

"Everything okay?" I ventured.

And then, just for one moment, she cried, miserably, achingly, as I'd seen little girls cry. And then she stopped. "You're a man, Elijah. How would you feel if your wife had to come to your office and smooth things over because you'd been ranting at your colleagues and tossing files around the room?"

I said that I'd feel awful but that I guess it would depend a bit on why I was in that state in the first place.

"You were in that state because *your brain was rotting. That's why!*"

She wept once more, but again just for an instant.

"Sorry if I'm not understanding, but are you saying that Lennie has a neurological disease?"

"Yes, I am saying that. He has FTD, frontal temporal dementia. His brain is going to pieces. He'll go senile and the kids might have the rogue gene too."

I tried to put a hand on her shoulder but she brushed it away and wiped her eyes.

I asked, "Is this why he's so angry, because he knows he's heading for dementia?"

"Partly. But his personality has changed. The disease does that. It changes people's personality. He's not the man I married. I married a nice guy."

I was about to say how sorry I was when she chirped, "Hey, look at those dogs! Never seen them before. What a hoot!"

Two drenched labradors, water flying off their coats, were playing tug-of-war with an old piece of rope, snarling ferociously and jerking their heads from side to side, hind legs driving into the sand for leverage.

"*Marvellous!*" I agreed, and we stood watching the tussle for a few minutes before continuing up the beach.

Then suddenly she said, "I can't do this anymore. See you next time." And she cut up the beach to a path that ran between two massive houses to the road.

\*

I heard nothing from her for days and didn't expect to. Now that she'd opened up to me, I fully expected to be cast into outer darkness.

Needing out for a while, I drove with Josh to see my sister Milly in Vermont.

I think maybe I feel more comfortable with Milly than with anyone in the world. She's the most sweetly solicitous listener I know, her dark grey-threaded hair framing caring brown eyes. As usual, I was spilling the existential beans – the soullessness of "Trumpite" Florida, the depression, the pointlessness, the isolation, the failure of the marriage. I didn't mention Jill.

"You know," Milly said, "you did a smart thing trying a different life after the cancer but maybe this was the wrong plan. How do you expect to haul yourself up when you don't know a soul down there and you haven't got anyone to share your intellectual interests with? Are you sure it wouldn't be better to cut your losses and go back to New York?"

"Judy would welcome me with open pincers."

"You know what I think about Judy. She's basically a really nice person and I've never been convinced that the marriage is as broken as you say."

"It hung by a thread from the very beginning," I said, quite forgetting those early years of erotic bliss and mutual fascination.

Milly herself had been married for twenty-five years. Her husband, an architect, had always been a bit aloof, but we took them for a quietly companionable and contented childless couple with shared interests, a lovely tasteful home and calm domestic routines. Then one day a piece of something broke off from an artery and went straight to his brain. The doctors told her he would have been dead when he hit the ground.

So I was surprised to hear her say, "All marriages hang by a thread. It's just a matter of the elasticity of the thread."

"And luck," I added. "Whether someone meets someone else."

"Yes, that too."

\*

As Josh and I re-entered Florida, the depression, which dreaded change as much as it needed it, morphed into nameless anxiety. I'd texted Jill a couple of times from Portland, got no reply, and was going to avoid that situation for the moment.

Next day I walked Josh to Starbucks. I took a local paper from a table and sat down with my coffee. The lead item read:

LOCAL LAWYER AND FATHER OF THREE
FOUND DEAD

Respected local lawyer and community leader, Leonard Corbett, was found dead yesterday.

He had apparently died in the front seat of his car which was parked at the Nona Velda scenic lookout. There appear to be no suspicious circumstances. Mr. Corbett, 53, leaves behind …

I tried to picture Jill getting the news but couldn't. My mind travelled back to that first meeting with her and then to that awful walk with Lenny. And then I seemed to disconnect and drift because when Josh snapped me back with a puzzled whimper, a good deal of time seemed to have passed. I took the phone from my pocket and typed: "I have just seen the news and am terribly sorry. No need to reply to this but if for any reason at any time you would like to get in touch please don't hesitate."

She did not get in touch but I thought about her, wondering how she was coping with the shock – if indeed it had come as a shock – and what longer-term effect this awful event might have on her.

If I said the whole thing deepened my own gloom, I'd be lying. There was a change, as if something within had loosened its grip just a touch and things, ever so slowly, were starting to shift. I thought I'd been about as low as you could go, yet I never thought of suicide. Things had got so bad for this guy that he'd killed himself, leaving his nice wife and children in a sort of misery which would go on forever. His misery, though, was over.

After a week I sent another text. No reply. Thinking that Jill might be walking on the beach, and not particularly wanting to see her if she did, I returned to the golf course walk, pausing with Josh cradled in my arms to watch alligators sunning themselves beside ponds and waterways, and giant herons stalking daintily in the shallows before striking with lightning speed.

Eventually we returned to the beach. It was bustling with balmy life, people sitting in chairs sipping drinks under umbrellas, kids chasing balls or digging in the wet sand among the entranced tooth fossickers, swimmers bobbing and nattering or stroking through the water where the fisherman had hooked and released his grotesque prey, and of course the dogs hurtling and swerving, or flying into the flat blue-green water after tennis balls or sticks.

Then one day I saw her. The dogs met excitedly. She walked determinedly towards me making steady, unsmiling eye contact, then stopped right in front of me. Just fleetingly, I had the remarkably selfish thought that now for the first time she looked like someone I could really connect with. She said nothing, so I stammered, "I really am terribly sorry. It must be beyond anything."

Still she said nothing, but looked at me with an expression that I have never been able to fathom from that day to this.

After another silence I tried again: "Look, I know …" but she flared at me, her face reddening. "I don't want to *talk about it!* Don't you *get it?!*"

I mumbled that of course I hoped I did get it and that I was sorry if …

Through tight lips she mumbled, "Sorry," and brushed past me, Jinx sensing that he should follow.

*

I never saw her again. A few months later I moved back to New York where I rented an apartment two blocks from Judy and tried to start over once again. This time it went somewhat better. Maybe the right amount of distance makes the heart grow fonder? Maybe I'd got to grips with a few things, like cancer in a gonad telling me I'm mortal. Like learning the difference between feeling like the living dead and wanting to die.

But sometimes I'd find myself combing the web for traces of that woman in Florida. After several searches I came upon this:

PET FRIENDLY REAL ESTATE SOLUTIONS
JILL CORBETT

And there she was, holding Jinx and smiling broadly, her hair cascading from a MAGA hat down those athletic shoulders and over a white Indian shirt and necklace. The necklace was threaded with what looked like alternating pearls and shards of ivory.

I gazed at the image for a long time, my soul setting itself against a current running swiftly south.

## About the author

Richard Freadman is Emeritus Professor of English at La Trobe University, and Adjunct Professor at Swinburne University where he is affiliated with the Wellbeing Clinic for Older Adults. In addition to his literary activities, he teaches and facilitates client life-writing in healthcare settings. His books include two volumes of memoir. He is married with three children and lives in Melbourne. *High Noon at Starbucks* is his first volume of fiction.

## Acknowledgments

I am grateful to the following who spent a lot of time commenting on versions of these stories:

Roger Averill, Hermi Burns, John Gatt-Rutter, Van Ikin and Mike Salzberg. For valuable responses along the way, thanks to Dianne Clifton, Susan Midalia and Iain Topliss.

Thanks to Maddie Freadman for her her much-needed and expert help with proofing.

Thanks also to Anna and Louis at Hybrid Publishers for their patient and expert work, and to Grant Gittus for the cover design.